Snow Country

Yasunari Kawabata (1899–1972), one of Japan's most distinguished writers, devoted his novels largely to aspects of love. Born in Osaka to wealthy parents, as a boy he hoped to become a painter, an aspiration later reflected in his novels. But his first stories were published while he was still in high school, and he decided to become a writer. After his graduation from Tokyo Imperial University in 1924, he quickly went to the forefront of modern Japanese writing.

Edward G. Seidensticker was born in Castle Rock, Colorado, in 1921. He received his BA from the University of Colorado, his MA from Columbia University, and did graduate work at both Harvard and Tokyo universities. In June 1942, Seidensticker enrolled at the US Navy Japanese Language School in Boulder, graduating with a burgeoning command of Japanese that would become the basis of his academic career as a translator of Japanese literature, including works by Tanizaki, Kawabata, Mishima and Kafu, and the daunting *The Tale of Genji*. In the 1950s, he taught at Sophia University in Tokyo for four years, returning to the US at the invitation of Stanford in 1962. After Stanford, Seidensticker taught at Michigan and Columbia, from which he retired in 1985.

Snow Country

by Yasunari Kawabata

Winner of the Nobel Prize for Literature

Translated, with an Introduction by
Edward G. Seidensticker

TUTTLE PUBLISHING
Tokyo • Rutland, Vermont • Singapore

UNESCO COLLECTION OF REPRESENTATIVE WORKS
JAPANESE SERIES

This book has been accepted in the Japanese Series of the Translations Collection of the United Nations Educational, Scientific and Cultural Organization (UNESCO).

Originally published in Japanese as *Yukiguni*

This novel, selected by the international PEN Club, has been translated with the assistance of UNESCO. The translation has been approved by the author.

Published by Tuttle Publishing, an imprint of Periplus Editions (HK) Ltd. by special arrangement with Alfred A. Knopf, Inc., New York

ISBN 4-8053-0635-1 (for sale in Japan only)

First Tuttle edition, 1957

Printed in Singapore

Distributed by:

Japan
Tuttle Publishing
Yaekari Building, 3rd Floor
5-4-12 Osaki, Shinagawa-ku
Tokyo 141-0032
Tel: (03) 5437 0171; Fax: (03) 5437 0755
Email: tuttle-sales@gol.com

Asia Pacific
Berkeley Books Pte. Ltd.
130 Joo Seng Road, #06-01/03
Singapore 368357
Tel: (65) 6280 1330; Fax: (65) 6280 6290
Email: inquiries@periplus.com.sg
www.periplus.com.sg

10 09 08 07 06
53 52 51 50

TUTTLE PUBLISHING® is a registered trademark of Tuttle Publishing.

INTRODUCTION

IN THE WINTER, cold winds blow down from Siberia, pick up moisture over the Japan Sea, and drop it as snow when they strike the mountains of Japan. The west coast of the main island of Japan is probably for its latitude (roughly, from Cape Hatteras to New York, or from Spanish Morocco to Barcelona) the snowiest region in the world. From December to April or May only the railroads are open, and the snow in the mountains is sometimes as much as fifteen feet deep.

The expression "snow country," then, does not mean simply country where snow falls. It means very specifically the part of the main island that lies west of the central mountain range. It suggests long, gray winters, tunnels under the snow, dark houses with rafters black from the smoke of winter fires—and perhaps chilblains, or, to the more imaginative, life divorced from time through the long snowbound months.

The hot springs, one of which is the locale of *Snow Country*, also have a peculiarly Japanese significance. The Japanese seldom goes to a hot spring for his health, and he never goes for "the season," as people once went to Bath or Saratoga. He may ski or view maple leaves or cherry blossoms, but his wife is usually not with him. The special delights of the hot spring are for the unaccompanied gentleman. No prosperous hot spring is without its geisha and its compliant hotel maids.

If the hot-spring geisha is not a social outcast, she is perilously near being one. The city geisha may become a celebrated musician or dancer, a political intriguer, even a dispenser of patronage. The hot-spring geisha must go on entertaining week-end guests, and the pretense that she is an artist and not a prostitute is often a thin one indeed. It is true that she sometimes marries an old guest, or persuades him to open a restaurant for her; but the possibility that she will drift from one hot spring to another, more unwanted with each change, makes her a particularly poignant symbol of wasted, decaying beauty.

It is not by chance that Kawabata Yasunari has chosen a hot-spring geisha for the heroine and the dark snow country for the setting of this novel. Darkness and wasted beauty run like a ground bass through his major work, and in *Snow Country* we perhaps feel most strongly the cold loneliness of the Kawabata world.

Kawabata was born near Osaka in 1899 and was orphaned at the age of two. His short stories began to attract attention soon after his graduation from Tokyo Imperial University. He presently became a leading figure in the lyrical school that offered the chief opposition to the proletarian literature of the late twenties. *Snow Country* was begun in 1934 and published piecemeal between 1935 and 1937. In 1947 a final installment was added, and the novel completed as it stands today.

Kawabata has been put, I think rightly, in a literary line that can be traced back to seventeenth-century *haiku* masters. *Haiku* are tiny seventeen-syllable poems that seek to convey a sudden awareness of beauty by a mating of opposite or incongruous terms. Thus the classical *haiku* characteristically fuses motion and stillness. Similarly Kawabata relies very heavily on a mingling of the senses. In *Snow Country* we come upon the roaring silence of a winter night, for instance, or the round softness of the sound of running water, or, in a somewhat more elaborate figure, the sound of a bell, far back in the singing of a teakettle, suddenly becomes a woman's feet. In the best of the dialogue, one brief sentence, often a *double-entendre,* is exchanged for another, much as characters in Japanese romances converse by exchanging brief poems.

The *haiku* manner presents a great challenge to the novelist. The manner is notable for its terseness and austerity, so that his novel must rather be like a series of brief flashes in a void. In *Snow Country* Kawabata has chosen a theme that makes a meeting between *haiku* and the novel possible. The hero is a wealthy dilettante quite incapable of love, and the heroine a hot-spring geisha, clean in the midst of corruption and yet somehow decaying before our eyes. The two try to love, but love can never bring them together. The nearer they are the farther apart they are. Shimamura, the hero, has built himself a half-cynical, half-wishful dream world, occupied by very little that suggests flesh and blood. He is an expert on the occidental ballet, but he has never seen a ballet. Indeed we are given cause to suspect that he would close his eyes if a ballet were set down in front of him. His love affair with Komako, the geisha, is doomed from the start. Through her he is drawn to Yoko, a strange, intense girl who, in Kawabata's image, glows like a light off in the mountain darkness; but he can take neither Komako nor Yoko as a per-

son. They can bring him no nearer their humanity
or his own, and he presently knows that the time
has come for him to leave.

Komako, for her part, has missed none of this.
"You're a good girl," Shimamura says affection-
ately in the climactic scene of the novel. But when,
a moment later, he unconsciously shifts to "You're
a good woman," she sees that she has been used.
She too knows that he must leave. It would be
hard to think of another novel in which so slight a
shift in tone reveals so much.

The final scene only brings the inevitable. We
know, as Komako staggers from the burning warehouse with Yoko in her arms, that Komako and
Shimamura have parted. Shimamura will go back
to the city and continue to play the cold dilettante,
while Komako will, as she herself has said, "go
pleasantly to seed" in the mountains. Yoko is the
burden she must bear, and the burden is made
heavier by the fact that the two women have twice
been rivals in love, once, in a way never clearly de-
fined for us, with the dying Yukio, again with
Shimamura. Little of this is stated directly. We
are not even told whether Yoko is alive or dead at
the end of the novel. If the reader finds the last
few pages puzzling, however, he should remember
that everything has already been implicitly suggested. The novel has in effect ended with Shima-

mura listening to the sound of the bell in the tea-kettle. The fire scene, beautifully written though it is, only emphasizes a point that has already been made.

Snow Country is perhaps Kawabata's master-piece. He has found in Shimamura's love affair the perfect symbol for a denial of love, and he has in the woman Komako and in the shadowy beauty of the snow country fit subjects for the haiku-like flashes that bring the denial forth. And, in the final analysis, the very success of the novel becomes a sort of affirmation of the humanity that is being denied.

E.G.S.

SNOW
COUNTRY

❦ ❦ ❦

PART ONE

THE TRAIN came out of the long tunnel into the snow country. The earth lay white under the night sky. The train pulled up at a signal stop.

A girl who had been sitting on the other side of the car came over and opened the window in front of Shimamura. The snowy cold poured in. Leaning far out the window, the girl called to the station master as though he were a great distance away.

The station master walked slowly over the snow,

a lantern in his hand. His face was buried to the nose in a muffler, and the flaps of his cap were turned down over his ears.

It's that cold, is it, thought Shimamura. Low, barracklike buildings that might have been railway dormitories were scattered here and there up the frozen slope of the mountain. The white of the snow fell away into the darkness some distance before it reached them.

"How are you?" the girl called out. "It's Yoko."

"Yoko, is it. On your way back? It's gotten cold again."

"I understand my brother has come to work here. Thank you for all you've done."

"It will be lonely, though. This is no place for a young boy."

"He's really no more than a child. You'll teach him what he needs to know, won't you."

"Oh, but he's doing very well. We'll be busier from now on, with the snow and all. Last year we had so much that the trains were always being stopped by avalanches, and the whole town was kept busy cooking for them."

"But look at the warm clothes, would you. My brother said in his letter that he wasn't even wearing a sweater yet."

"I'm not warm unless I have on four layers, myself. The young ones start drinking when it gets cold, and the first thing you know they're over there in bed with colds." He waved his lantern toward the dormitories.

"Does my brother drink?"

"Not that I know of."

"You're on your way home now, are you?"

"I had a little accident. I've been going to the doctor."

"You must be more careful."

The station master, who had an overcoat on over his kimono, turned as if to cut the freezing conversation short. "Take care of yourself," he called over his shoulder.

"Is my brother here now?" Yoko looked out over the snow-covered platform. "See that he behaves himself." It was such a beautiful voice that it struck one as sad. In all its high resonance it seemed to come echoing back across the snowy night.

The girl was still leaning out the window when the train pulled away from the station. "Tell my brother to come home when he has a holiday," she called out to the station master, who was walking along the tracks.

"I'll tell him," the man called back.

Yoko closed the window and pressed her hands to her red cheeks.

Three snowplows were waiting for the heavy snows here on the Border Range. There was an electric avalanche-warning system at the north and south entrances to the tunnel. Five thousand workers were ready to clear away the snow, and two thousand young men from the volunteer fire-departments could be mobilized if they were needed.

Yoko's brother would be working at this signal stop, so soon to be buried under the snow—somehow that fact made the girl more interesting to Shimamura.

"The girl"—something in her manner suggested the unmarried girl. Shimamura of course had no way of being sure what her relationship was to the man with her. They acted rather like a married couple. The man was clearly ill, however, and illness shortens the distance between a man and a woman. The more earnest the ministrations, the more the two come to seem like husband and wife. A girl taking care of a man far older than she, for all the world like a young mother, can from a distance be taken for his wife.

But Shimamura in his mind had cut the girl off from the man with her and decided from her general appearance and manner that she was unmarried. And then, because he had been looking at her from a strange angle for so long, emotions peculiarly his own had perhaps colored his judgment.

It had been three hours earlier. In his boredom,

Shimamura stared at his left hand as the forefinger bent and unbent. Only this hand seemed to have a vital and immediate memory of the woman he was going to see. The more he tried to call up a clear picture of her, the more his memory failed him, the farther she faded away, leaving him nothing to catch and hold. In the midst of this uncertainty only the one hand, and in particular the forefinger, even now seemed damp from her touch, seemed to be pulling him back to her from afar. Taken with the strangeness of it, he brought the hand to his face, then quickly drew a line across the misted-over window. A woman's eye floated up before him. He almost called out in his astonishment. But he had been dreaming, and when he came to himself he saw that it was only the reflection in the window of the girl opposite. Outside it was growing dark, and the lights had been turned on in the train, transforming the window into a mirror. The mirror had been clouded over with steam until he drew that line across it.

The one eye by itself was strangely beautiful, but, feigning a traveler's weariness and putting his face to the window as if to look at the scenery outside, he cleared the steam from the rest of the glass.

The girl leaned attentively forward, looking down at the man before her. Shimamura could see from the way her strength was gathered in her shoulders that the suggestion of fierceness in her eyes was but a sign of an intentness that did not permit her to blink. The man lay with his head pillowed at the window and his legs bent so that his feet were on the seat facing, beside the girl. It was a third-class coach. The pair were not directly opposite Shimamura but rather one seat forward, and the man's head showed in the window-mirror only as far as the ear.

Since the girl was thus diagonally opposite him, Shimamura could as well have looked directly at her. When the two of them came on the train, however, something coolly piercing about her beauty had startled Shimamura, and as he hastily lowered his eyes he had seen the man's ashen fingers clutching at the girl's. Somehow it seemed wrong to look their way again.

The man's face in the mirror suggested the feeling of security and repose it gave him to be able to rest his eyes on the girl's breast. His very weakness lent a certain soft balance and harmony to the two figures. One end of his scarf served as a pillow, and the other end, pulled up tight over his mouth like a mask, rested on his cheek. Now and then it fell loose or slipped down over his nose, and almost before he had time to signal his annoyance the girl gently rearranged it. The process was repeated over and over, automatically, so often that Shimamura, watching them, almost found himself growing impatient. Occasionally the bottom of the overcoat in which the man's feet were wrapped would slip open and fall to the floor, and the girl would quickly pull it back together. It was all completely natural, as if the two of them, quite insensitive to space, meant to go on forever, farther and farther into the distance. For Shimamura there was none of the pain that the sight of something truly sad can bring. Rather it was as if he were watching a tableau in a dream—and that was no doubt the working of his strange mirror.

In the depths of the mirror the evening landscape moved by, the mirror and the reflected figures like motion pictures superimposed one on the other. The figures and the background were unrelated, and yet the figures, transparent and intangible, and the background, dim in the gathering darkness, melted together into a sort of symbolic world not of this world. Particularly when a light out in the mountains shone in the center of the girl's face, Shimamura felt his chest rise at the inexpressible beauty of it.

The mountain sky still carried traces of evening red. Individual shapes were clear far into the distance, but the monotonous mountain landscape, undistinguished for mile after mile, seemed all the

more undistinguished for having lost its last traces
of color. There was nothing in it to catch the eye,
and it seemed to flow along in a wide, unformed
emotion. That was of course because the girl's face
was floating over it. Cut off by the face, the evening landscape moved steadily by around its outlines. The face too seemed transparent—but was it
really transparent? Shimamura had the illusion that
the evening landscape was actually passing over the
face, and the flow did not stop to let him be sure it
was not.

The light inside the train was not particularly
strong, and the reflection was not as clear as it
would have been in a mirror. Since there was no
glare, Shimamura came to forget that it was a mirror he was looking at. The girl's face seemed to be
out in the flow of the evening mountains.

It was then that a light shone in the face. The
reflection in the mirror was not strong enough to
blot out the light outside, nor was the light strong
enough to dim the reflection. The light moved
across the face, though not to light it up. It was a
distant, cold light. As it sent its small ray through
the pupil of the girl's eye, as the eye and the light
were superimposed one on the other, the eye became a weirdly beautiful bit of phosphorescence on
the sea of evening mountains.

There was no way for Yoko to know that she was being stared at. Her attention was concentrated on the sick man, and even had she looked toward Shimamura, she would probably not have seen her reflection, and she would have paid no attention to the man looking out the window.

It did not occur to Shimamura that it was improper to stare at the girl so long and stealthily. That too was no doubt because he was taken by the unreal, otherworldly power of his mirror in the evening landscape.

When, therefore, the girl called out to the station master, her manner again suggesting overearnestness, Shimamura perhaps saw her first of all as rather like a character out of an old, romantic tale.

The window was dark by the time they came to the signal stop. The charm of the mirror faded with the fading landscape. Yoko's face was still there, but for all the warmth of her ministrations, Shimamura had found in her a transparent coldness. He did not clear the window as it clouded over again.

He was startled, then, when a half-hour later Yoko and the man got off the train at the same station as he. He looked around as though he were about to be drawn into something, but the cold air on the platform made him suddenly ashamed of his rudeness on the train. He crossed the tracks in front of the locomotive without looking back again.

The man, clinging to Yoko's shoulder, was about to climb down to the tracks from the platform opposite when from this side a station attendant raised a hand to stop them.

A long freight train came out of the darkness to block them from sight.

The porter from the inn was so well-equipped for the cold that he suggested a fireman. He had on ear flaps and high rubber boots. The woman looking out over the tracks from the waiting-room wore a blue cape with the cowl pulled over her head.

Shimamura, still warm from the train, was not sure how cold it really was. This was his first taste of the snow-country winter, however, and he felt somewhat intimidated.

"Is it as cold as all that?"

"We're ready for the winter. It's always especially cold the night it clears after a snow. It must be below freezing tonight."

"This is below freezing, is it?" Shimamura looked up at the delicate icicles along the eaves as he climbed into the taxi. The white of the snow made the deep eaves look deeper still, as if everything had sunk quietly into the earth.

"The cold here is different, though, that's easy

to see. It feels different when you touch something."

"Last year it went down to zero."

"How much snow?"

"Ordinarily seven or eight feet, sometimes as much as twelve or thirteen, I'd say."

"The heavy snows come from now on?"

"They're just beginning. We had about a foot, but it's melted down a good bit."

"It's been melting, has it?"

"We could have a heavy snow almost any time now, though."

It was the beginning of December.

Shimamura's nose had been stopped up by a stubborn cold, but it cleared to the middle of his head in the cold air, and began running as if the matter in it were washing cleanly away.

"Is the girl who lived with the music teacher still around?"

"She's still around. You didn't see her in the station? In the dark-blue cape?"

"So that's who it was. We can call her later, I suppose?"

"This evening?"

"This evening."

"I hear the music teacher's son came back on your train. She was at the station to meet him."

The sick man he had watched in that evening

mirror, then, was the son of the music teacher in whose house the woman Shimamura had come to see was living.

He felt a current pass through him, and yet the coincidence did not seem especially remarkable. Indeed he was surprised at himself for being so little surprised.

Somewhere in his heart Shimamura saw a question, as clearly as if it were standing there before him: was there something, what would happen, between the woman his hand remembered and the woman in whose eye that mountain light had glowed? Or had he not yet shaken off the spell of the evening landscape in that mirror? He wondered whether the flowing landscape was not perhaps symbolic of the passage of time.

The hot-spring inn had its fewest guests in the weeks before the skiing season began, and by the time Shimamura had come up from the bath the place seemed to be asleep. The glass doors rattled slightly each time he took a step down the sagging corridor. At the end, where it turned past the office, he saw the tall figure of the woman, her skirts trailing coldly off across the dark floor.

He started back as he saw the long skirts—had

she finally become a geisha? She did not come toward him, she did not bend in the slightest movement of recognition. From the distance he caught something intent and serious in the still form. He hurried up to her, but they said nothing even when he was beside her. She started to smile through the thick, white geisha's powder. Instead she melted into tears, and the two of them walked off silently toward his room.

In spite of what had passed between them, he had not written to her, or come to see her, or sent her the dance instructions he had promised. She was no doubt left to think that he had laughed at her and forgotten her. It should therefore have been his part to begin with an apology or an excuse, but as they walked along, not looking at each other, he could tell that, far from blaming him, she had room in her heart only for the pleasure of regaining what had been lost. He knew that if he spoke he would only make himself seem the more wanting in seriousness. Overpowered by the woman, he walked along wrapped in a soft happiness. Abruptly, at the foot of the stairs, he shoved his left fist before her eyes, with only the forefinger extended.

"This remembered you best of all."

"Oh?" The woman took the finger in her hand and clung to it as though to lead him upstairs.

She let go his hand as they came to the *kotatsu**
in his room, and suddenly she was red from her
forehead to her throat. As if to conceal her confusion, she clutched at his hand again.

"This remembered me?"

"Not the right hand. This." He pushed his right
hand into the *kotatsu* to warm it, and again gave her
his left fist with the finger extended.

"I know." Her face carefully composed, she
laughed softly. She opened his hand, and pressed
her cheek against it. "This remembered me?"

"Cold! I don't think I've ever touched such cold
hair."

"Is there snow in Tokyo yet?"

"You remember what you said then? But you
were wrong. Why else would anyone come to such
a place in December?"

"Then": the danger of avalanches was over, and
the season for climbing mountains in the spring
green had come.

Presently the new sprouts would be gone from
the table.

Shimamura, who lived a life of idleness, found

---

* A charcoal brazier covered by a wooden frame and a
quilt. Although it warms little more than the hands and feet,
the *kotatsu* is the only heating device in the ordinary Japanese
house.

that he tended to lose his honesty with himself, and he frequently went out alone into the mountains to recover something of it. He had come down to the hot-spring village after seven days in the Border Range. He asked to have a geisha called. Unfortunately, however, there was a celebration that day in honor of the opening of a new road, the maid said, so lively a celebration that the town's combined cocoon-warehouse and theater had been taken over, and the twelve or thirteen geisha had more than enough to keep them busy. The girl who lived at the music teacher's might come, though. She sometimes helped at parties, but she would have gone home after no more than one or two dances. As Shimamura questioned her, the maid told him more about the girl at the music teacher's: the samisen and dancing teacher had living with her a girl who was not a geisha but who was sometimes asked to help at large parties. Since there were no young apprentice geisha in the town, and since most of the local geisha were at an age when they preferred not to have to dance, the services of the girl were much valued. She almost never came alone to entertain a guest at the inn, and yet she could not exactly be called an amateur—such in general was the maid's story.

An odd story, Shimamura said to himself, and dismissed the matter. An hour or so later, however, the woman from the music teacher's came in with the maid. Shimamura brought himself up straight. The maid started to leave but was called back by the woman.

The impression the woman gave was a wonderfully clean and fresh one. It seemed to Shimamura that she must be clean to the hollows under her toes. So clean indeed did she seem that he wondered whether his eyes, back from looking at early summer in the mountains, might not be deceiving him.

There was something about her manner of dress that suggested the geisha, but she did not have the trailing geisha skirts. On the contrary, she wore her soft, unlined summer kimono with an emphasis on careful propriety. The *obi** seemed expensive, out of keeping with the kimono, and struck him as a little sad.

The maid slipped out as they started talking about the mountains. The woman was not very sure of the names of the mountains that could be seen from the inn, and, since Shimamura did not feel the urge to drink that might have come to him in the company of an ordinary geisha, she began telling of her past in a surprisingly matter-of-fact way. She was born in this snow country, but she had been put under contract as a geisha in Tokyo. Presently

* The sash with which a kimono is tied. A woman's *obi* is wide and stiff, a man's narrower and usually softer.

she found a patron who paid her debts for her and proposed to set her up as a dancing teacher, but unfortunately a year and a half later he died. When it came to the story of what had happened since, the story of what was nearest to her, she was less quick to tell her secrets. She said she was nineteen. Shimamura had taken her to be twenty-one or twenty-two, and, since he assumed that she was not lying, the knowledge that she had aged beyond her years gave him for the first time a little of the ease he expected to feel with a geisha. When they began talking of the Kabuki, he found that she knew more about actors and styles than he did. She talked on feverishly, as though she had been starved for someone who would listen to her, and presently began to show an ease and abandon that revealed her to be at heart a woman of the pleasure quarters after all. And she seemed in general to know what there was to know about men. Shimamura, however, had labeled her an amateur and, after a week in the mountains during which he had spoken to almost no one, he found himself longing for a companion. It was therefore friendship more than anything else that he felt for the woman. His response to the mountains had extended itself to cover her.

On her way to the bath the next afternoon, she left her towel and soap in the hall and came in to talk to him.

She had barely taken a seat when he asked her to call him a geisha.

"Call you a geisha?"

"You know what I mean."

"I didn't come to be asked that." She stood up abruptly and went over to the window, her face reddening as she looked out at the mountains. "There are no women like that here."

"Don't be silly."

"It's the truth." She turned sharply to face him, and sat down on the window sill. "No one forces a geisha to do what she doesn't want to. It's entirely up to the geisha herself. That's one service the inn won't provide for you. Go ahead, try calling someone and talking to her yourself, if you want to."

"You call someone for me."

"Why do you expect me to do that?"

"I'm thinking of you as a friend. That's why I've behaved so well."

"And this is what you call being a friend?" Led on by his manner, she had become engagingly child-like. But a moment later she burst out: "Isn't it fine that you think you can ask me a thing like that!"

"What is there to be so excited about? I'm too healthy after a week in the mountains, that's all. I keep having the wrong ideas. I can't even sit here talking to you the way I would like to."

The woman was silent, her eyes on the floor. Shimamura had come to a point where he knew he was only parading his masculine shamelessness, and yet it seemed likely enough that the woman was familiar with the failing and need not be shocked by it. He looked at her. Perhaps it was the rich lashes of the downcast eyes that made her face seem warm and sensuous. She shook her head very slightly, and again a faint blush spread over her face.

"Call any geisha you like."

"But isn't that exactly what I'm asking you to do? I've never been here before, and I've no idea which geisha are the best-looking."

"What do you consider good-looking?"

"Someone young. You're less apt to make mistakes when they're young. And someone who doesn't talk too much. Clean, and not too quick. When I want someone to talk to, I can talk to you."

"I'll not come again."

"Don't be foolish."

"I said I'll not come again. Why should I come again?"

"But haven't I told you it's exactly because I want to be friends with you that I've behaved so well?"

"You've said enough."

"Suppose I were to go too far with you. Very

probably from tomorrow I wouldn't want to talk to you. I couldn't stand the sight of you. I've had to come into the mountains to want to talk to people again, and I've left you alone so that I can talk to you. And what about yourself? You can't be too careful with travelers."

"That's true."

"Of course it is. Think of yourself. If it were a woman you objected to, you wouldn't want to see me afterwards. It would be much better for her to be a woman you picked out."

"I don't want to hear any more." She turned sharply away, but presently she added: "I suppose there's something in what you say."

"An affair of the moment, no more. Nothing beautiful about it. You know that—it couldn't last."

"That's true. It's that way with everyone who comes here. This is a hot spring and people are here for a day or two and gone." Her manner was remarkably open—the transition had been almost too abrupt. "The guests are mostly travelers. I'm still just a child myself, but I've listened to all the talk. The guest who doesn't say he's fond of you, and yet you somehow know is—he's the one you have pleasant memories of. You don't forget him, even long after he's left you, they say. And he's the one you get letters from."

She stood up from the window sill and took a seat on the mat below it. She seemed to be living in the past, and yet she seemed to be very near Shima-mura.

Her voice carried such a note of immediate feeling that he felt a little guilty, as though he had deceived her too easily.

He had not been lying, though. To him this woman was an amateur. His desire for a woman was not of a sort to make him want this particular woman—it was something to be taken care of lightly and with no sense of guilt. This woman was too clean. From the moment he saw her, he had separated this woman and the other in his mind.

Then too, he had been trying to decide where he would go to escape the summer heat, and it occurred to him that he could bring his family to this mountain hot spring. The woman, being fortunately an amateur, would be a good companion for his wife. He might even have his wife take dancing lessons to keep from getting bored. He was quite serious about it. He said he felt only friendship for the woman, but he had his reasons for thus stepping into shallow water without taking the final plunge.

And something like that evening mirror was no doubt at work here too. He disliked the thought of drawn-out complications from an affair with a woman whose position was so ambiguous; but beyond that he saw her as somehow unreal, like the woman's face in that evening mirror.

His taste for the occidental dance had much the same air of unreality about it. He had grown up in the merchants' section of Tokyo, and he had been thoroughly familiar with the Kabuki theater from his childhood. As a student his interests had shifted to the Japanese dance and the dance-drama. Never satisfied until he learned everything about his subject, he had taken to searching through old documents and visiting the heads of various dance schools, and presently he had made friends with rising figures in the dance world and was writing what one might call research pieces and critical essays. It was but natural, then, that he should come to feel a keen dissatisfaction with the slumbering old tradition as well as with reformers who sought only to please themselves. Just as he had arrived at the conclusion that there was nothing for it but to throw himself actively into the dance movement, and as he was being persuaded to do so by certain of the younger figures in the dance world, he abruptly switched to the occidental dance. He stopped seeing the Japanese dance. He gathered pictures and descriptions of the occidental ballet, and began laboriously collecting programs and posters from abroad. This was more than simple fascina-

tion with the exotic and the unknown. The pleasure
he found in his new hobby came in fact from his
inability to see with his own eyes occidentals in
occidental ballets. There was proof of this in his
deliberate refusal to study the ballet as performed
by Japanese. Nothing could be more comfortable
than writing about the ballet from books. A ballet
he had never seen was an art in another world. It
was an unrivaled armchair reverie, a lyric from
some paradise. He called his work research, but it
was actually free, uncontrolled fantasy. He preferred not to savor the ballet in the flesh; rather he
savored the phantasms of his own dancing imagination, called up by Western books and pictures. It
was like being in love with someone he had never
seen. But it was also true that Shimamura, with no
real occupation, took some satisfaction from the
fact that his occasional introductions to the occidental dance put him on the edge of the literary
world—even while he was laughing at himself and
his work.

It might be said that his knowledge was now for
the first time in a very great while being put to use,
since talk of the dance helped bring the woman
nearer to him; and yet it was also possible that,
hardly knowing it, he was treating the woman exactly as he treated the occidental dance.

He felt a little guilty, as though he had deceived

her, when he saw how the frivolous words of the traveler who would be gone tomorrow seemed to have struck something deep and serious in the woman's life.

But he went on: "I can bring my family here, and we can all be friends."

"I understand that well enough." She smiled, her voice falling, and a touch of the geisha's playfulness came out. "I'd like that much better. It lasts longer if you're just friends."

"You'll call someone, then?"

"Now?"

"Now."

"But what can you say to a woman in broad daylight?"

"At night there's too much danger of getting the dregs no one else wants."

"You take this for a cheap hot-spring town like any other. I should think you could tell just from looking at the place." Her tone was sober again, as though she felt thoroughly degraded. She repeated with the same emphasis as before that there were no girls here of the sort he wanted. When Shimamura expressed his doubts, she flared up, then retreated a step. It was up to the geisha whether she would stay the night or not. If she stayed without permission from her house, it was her own responsibility. If she had permission the house took full responsibility, whatever happened. That was the difference.

"Full responsibility?"

"If there should happen to be a child, or some sort of disease."

Shimamura smiled wryly at the foolishness of his question. In a mountain village, though, the arrangements between a geisha and her keeper might indeed still be so easygoing. . . .

Perhaps with the idler's bent for protective coloring, Shimamura had an instinctive feeling for the spirit of the places he visited, and he had felt as he came down from the mountains that, for all its air of bare frugality, there was something comfortable and easy about the village. He heard at the inn that it was indeed one of the more comfortable villages in this harsh snow country. Until the railway was put through, only very recently, it had served mainly as a medicinal spring for farmers in the area. The house that kept geisha would generally have a faded shop curtain that advertised it as a restaurant or a tearoom, but a glance at the old-style sliding doors, their paper panels dark with age, made the passer-by suspect that guests were few. The shop that sold candy or everyday sundries might have its one geisha, and the owner would have his small farm besides the shop and the geisha.

Perhaps because she lived with the music teacher, there seemed to be no resentment at the fact that a woman not yet licensed as a geisha was now and then helping at parties.

"How many are there in all?"

"How many geisha? Twelve or thirteen, I suppose."

"Which one do you recommend?" Shimamura stood up to ring for the maid.

"You won't mind if I leave now."

"I mind very much indeed."

"I can't stay." She spoke as if trying to shake off the humiliation. "I'm going. It's all right. I don't mind. I'll come again."

When the maid came in, however, she sat down as though nothing were amiss. The maid asked several times which geisha she should call, but the woman refused to mention a name.

One look at the seventeen- or eighteen-year-old geisha who was presently led in, and Shimamura felt his need for a woman fall dully away. Her arms, with their underlying darkness, had not yet filled out, and something about her suggested an unformed, good-natured young girl. Shimamura, at pains not to show that his interest had left him, faced her dutifully, but he could not keep himself from looking less at her than at the new green on the mountains behind her. It seemed almost too much of an effort to talk. She was the mountain geisha through and through. He lapsed into a glum silence. No doubt thinking to be tactful and adroit, the woman stood up and left the room, and the conversation became still heavier. Even so, he managed to pass perhaps an hour with the geisha. Looking for a pretext to be rid of her, he remembered that he had had money telegraphed from Tokyo. He had to go to the post office before it closed, he said, and the two of them left the room.

But at the door of the inn he was seduced by the mountain, strong with the smell of new leaves. He started climbing roughly up it.

He laughed on and on, not knowing himself what was funny.

When he was pleasantly tired, he turned sharply around and, tucking the skirts of his kimono into his *obi*, ran headlong back down the slope. Two yellow butterflies flew up at his feet.

The butterflies, weaving in and out, climbed higher than the line of the Border Range, their yellow turning to white in the distance.

"What happened?" The woman was standing in the shade of the cedar trees. "You must have been very happy, the way you were laughing."

"I gave it up." Shimamura felt the same senseless laugh rising again. "I gave it up."

"Oh?" She turned and walked slowly into the grove. Shimamura followed in silence.

It was a shrine grove. The woman sat down on a flat rock beside the moss-covered shrine dogs.

"It's always cool here. Even in the middle of the summer there's a cool wind."

"Are all the geisha like that?"

"They're all a little like her, I suppose. Some of the older ones are very attractive, if you had wanted one of them." Her eyes were on the ground, and she spoke coldly. The dusky green of the cedars seemed to reflect from her neck.

Shimamura looked up at the cedar branches. "It's all over. My strength left me—really, it seems very funny."

From behind the rock, the cedars threw up their trunks in perfectly straight lines, so high that he could see the tops only by arching his back. The dark needles blocked out the sky, and the stillness seemed to be singing quietly. The trunk against which Shimamura leaned was the oldest of all. For some reason all the branches on the north side had withered, and, their tips broken and fallen, they looked like stakes driven into the trunk with their sharp ends out, to make a terrible weapon for some god.

"I made a mistake. I saw you as soon as I came down from the mountains, and I let myself think that all the geisha here were like you," he laughed. It occurred to him now that the thought of washing away in such short order the vigor of seven days in the mountains had perhaps first come to him when he saw the cleanness of this woman.

She gazed down at the river, distant in the afternoon sun. Shimamura was a little unsure of himself.

"I forgot," she suddenly remarked, with forced lightness. "I brought your tobacco. I went back up to your room a little while ago and found that you had gone out. I wondered where you could be, and then I saw you running up the mountain for all you were worth. I watched from the window. You were very funny. But you forgot your tobacco. Here."

She took the tobacco from her kimono sleeve and lighted a match for him.

"I wasn't very nice to that poor girl."

"But it's up to the guest, after all, when he wants to let the geisha go."

Through the quiet, the sound of the rocky river came up to them with a rounded softness. Shadows were darkening in the mountain chasms on the other side of the valley, framed in the cedar branches.

"Unless she were as good as you, I'd feel cheated when I saw you afterwards."

"Don't talk to me about it. You're just unwilling to admit you lost, that's all." There was scorn in her voice, and yet an affection of quite a new sort flowed between them.

As it became clear to Shimamura that he had from the start wanted only this woman, and that he had taken his usual roundabout way of saying so, he began to see himself as rather repulsive and the woman as all the more beautiful. Something from that cool figure had swept through him after she called to him from under the cedars.

The high, thin nose was a little lonely, a little sad, but the bud of her lips opened and closed smoothly, like a beautiful little circle of leeches. Even when she was silent her lips seemed always to be moving. Had they had wrinkles or cracks, or had their color been less fresh, they would have struck one as unwholesome, but they were never anything but smooth and shining. The line of her eyelids neither rose nor fell. As if for some special reason, it drew its way straight across her face. There was something faintly comical about the effect, but the short, thick hair of her eyebrows sloped gently down to enfold the line discreetly. There was nothing remarkable about the outlines of her round, slightly aquiline face. With her skin like white porcelain coated over a faint pink, and her throat still girlish, not yet filled out, the impression she gave was above all one of cleanness, not quite one of real beauty.

Her breasts were rather full for a woman used to the high, binding *obi* of the geisha.

"The sand flies have come out," she said, standing up and brushing at the skirt of her kimono.

Alone in the quiet, they could think of little to say.

It was perhaps ten o'clock that night. The woman called loudly to Shimamura from the hall, and a moment later she fell into his room as if someone had thrown her. She collapsed in front of the table. Flailing with a drunken arm at everything that happened to be on it, she poured herself a glass of water and drank in great gulps.

She had gone out to meet some travelers down from the mountains that evening, men she had been friendly with during the skiing season the winter before. They had invited her to the inn, whereupon they had had a riotous party, complete with geisha, and had proceeded to get her drunk.

Her head waved uncertainly, and she seemed prepared to talk on forever. Presently she remembered herself. "I shouldn't be here. I'll come again. They'll be looking for me. I'll come again later." She staggered from the room.

An hour or so later, he heard uneven steps coming down the long hall. She was weaving from side to side, he could tell, running into a wall, stumbling to the floor.

"Shimamura, Shimamura," she called in a high voice. "I can't see. Shimamura!"

It was, with no attempt at covering itself, the naked heart of a woman calling out to her man. Shimamura was startled. That high, piercing voice must surely be echoing all through the inn. He got up hastily. Pushing her fingers through the paper panel, the woman clutched at the frame of the door, and fell heavily against him.

"You're here." Clinging to him, she sank to the floor. She leaned against him as she spoke. "I'm not drunk. Who says I'm drunk? Ah, it hurts, it hurts. It's just that it hurts. I know exactly what I'm doing. Give me water, I want water. I mixed my drinks, that was my mistake. That's what goes to your head. It hurts. They had a bottle of cheap whisky. How was I to know it was cheap?" She rubbed her forehead with her fists.

The sound of the rain outside was suddenly louder.

Each time he relaxed his embrace even a little, she threatened to collapse. His arm was around her neck so tight that her hair was rumpled against his cheek. He thrust a hand inside the neck of her kimono.

He added coaxing words, but she did not answer. She folded her arms like a bar over the breast he was asking for.

"What's the matter with you." She bit savagely at her arm, as though angered by its refusal to serve her. "Damn you, damn you. Lazy, useless. What's the matter with you."

Shimamura drew back startled. There were deep teeth-marks on her arm.

She no longer resisted, however. Giving herself up to his hands, she began writing something with the tip of her finger. She would tell him the people she liked, she said. After she had written the names of some twenty or thirty actors, she wrote "Shimamura, Shimamura," over and over again.

The delicious swelling under Shimamura's hand grew warmer.

"Everything is all right." His voice was serene. "Everything is all right again." He sensed something a little motherly in her.

But the headache came back. She writhed and twisted, and sank to the floor in a corner of the room.

"It won't do. It won't do. I'm going home. Going home."

"Do you think you can walk that far? And listen to the rain."

"I'll go home barefoot. I'll crawl home."

"You don't think that's a little dangerous? If you have to go, I'll take you."

The inn was on a hill, and the road was a steep one.

"Suppose you try loosening your clothes. Lie down for a little while and you'll feel well enough to go."

"No, no. This is the way. I'm used to it." She sat up straight and took a deep breath, but breathing was clearly painful. She felt a little nauseated, she said, and opened the window behind her, but she could not vomit. She seemed to be holding back the urge to fall down writhing on the floor. Now and then she came to herself. "I'm going home, I'm going home," she said again and again, and presently it was after two.

"Go on to bed. Go on to bed when a person tells you to."

"But what will you do?" Shimamura asked.

"I'll just sit here like this. When I feel a little better I'll go home. I'll go home before daylight." She crawled over on her knees and tugged at him. "Go on to sleep. Pay no attention to me, I tell you."

Shimamura went back to bed. The woman sprawled over the table and took another drink of water.

"Get up. Get up when a person tells you to."

"Which do you want me to do?"

"All right, go to sleep."

"You aren't making much sense, you know." He pulled her into bed after him.

Her face was turned half away, hidden from him, but after a time she thrust her lips violently toward him.

Then, as if in a delirium she were trying to tell of her pain, she repeated over and over, he did not know how many times: "No, no. Didn't you say you wanted to be friends?"

The almost too serious tone of it rather dulled his ardor, and as he saw her wrinkle her forehead in the effort to control herself, he thought of standing by the commitment he had made.

But then she said: "I won't have any regrets. I'll never have any regrets. But I'm not that sort of woman. It can't last. Didn't you say so yourself?"

She was still half numb from the liquor.

"It's not my fault. It's yours. You lost. You're the weak one. Not I." She ran on almost in a trance, and she bit at her sleeve as if to fight back the happiness.

She was quiet for a time, apparently drained of feeling. Then, as if the thought came to her from somewhere in her memory, she struck out: "You're laughing, aren't you? You're laughing at me."

"I am not."

"Deep in your heart you're laughing at me. Even if you aren't now, you will be later." She was choked with tears. Turning away from him, she buried her face in her hands.

But a moment later she was calm again. Soft and yielding as if she were offering herself up, she was suddenly very intimate, and she began telling him all about herself. She seemed quite to have forgotten the headache. She said not a word about what had just happened.

"But I've been so busy talking I haven't noticed how late it is." She smiled a little bashfully. She had to leave before daylight, she said. "It's still dark. But people here get up early." Time after time she got up to look out the window. "They won't be able to see my face yet. And it's raining. No one will be going out to the fields this morning."

She seemed reluctant to go even when the lines of the mountain and of the roofs on its slopes were floating out of the rain. Finally it was time for the hotel maids to be up and about. She retouched her hair and ran, almost fled, from the room, brushing aside Shimamura's offer to see her to the door. Someone might catch a glimpse of the two of them together.

Shimamura went back to Tokyo that day.

.   .   .

"You remember what you said then? But you were wrong. Why else would anyone come to such a place in December? I wasn't laughing at you."

The woman raised her head. Her face where it had been pressed against Shimamura's hand was red under the thick powder, from the eye across the bridge of the nose. It made him think of the snow-country cold, and yet, because of the darkness of her hair, there was a certain warmth in it.

She smiled quietly, as though dazzled by a bright light. Perhaps, as she smiled, she thought of "then," and Shimamura's words gradually colored her whole body. When she bowed her head, a little stiffly, he could see that even her back under her kimono was flushed a deep red. Set off by the color of her hair, the moist sensuous skin was as if laid naked before him. Her hair could not really have been called thick. Stiff like a man's, and swept up into a high Japanese-style coiffure with not a hair out of place, it glowed like some heavy black stone.

Shimamura looked at the hair and wondered whether the coldness that had so startled him—he had never touched such cold hair, he said—might be less the cold of the snow-country winter than something in the hair itself. The woman began counting on her fingers. For some time she counted on.

"What are you counting?" he asked. Still the counting continued.

"It was the twenty-third of May."

"You're counting the days, are you. Don't forget that July and August are two long months in a row."

"It's the hundred-and-ninety-ninth day. It's exactly a hundred and ninety-nine days."

"How did you remember it was the twenty-third of May?"

"All I have to do is look in my diary."

"You keep a diary?"

"It's always fun to read an old diary. But I don't hide anything when I write in my diary, and sometimes I'm ashamed to look at it myself."

"When did you begin?"

"Just before I went to Tokyo as a geisha. I didn't have any money, and I bought a plain notebook for two or three sen and drew in lines. I must have had a very sharp pencil. The lines are all neat and close together, and every page is crammed from top to bottom. When I had enough money to buy a diary, it wasn't the same any more. I started taking things for granted. It's that way with my writing practice, too. I used to practice on newspapers before I even thought of trying good paper, but now I set it down on good paper from the start."

"And you've kept the diary all this time?"

"Yes. The year I was sixteen and this year have been the best. I write in my diary when I'm home from a party and ready for bed, and when I read it over I can see places where I've gone to sleep writing. . . . But I don't write every day. Some days I miss. Way off here in the mountains, every party's the same. This year I couldn't find anything except a diary with a new day on each page. It was a mistake. When I start writing, I want to write on and on."

But even more than at the diary, Shimamura was surprised at her statement that she had carefully catalogued every novel and short story she had read since she was fifteen or sixteen. The record already filled ten notebooks.

"You write down your criticisms, do you?"

"I could never do anything like that. I just write down the author and the characters and how they are related to each other. That is about all."

"But what good does it do?"

"None at all."

"A waste of effort."

"A complete waste of effort," she answered brightly, as though the admission meant little to her. She gazed solemnly at Shimamura, however.

A complete waste of effort. For some reason Shimamura wanted to stress the point. But, drawn to her at that moment, he felt a quiet like the voice of the rain flow over him. He knew well enough that for her it was in fact no waste of effort, but somehow the final determination that it was had the effect of distilling and purifying the woman's existence.

Her talk of novels seemed to have little to do with "literature" in the everyday sense of the word. The only friendly ties she had with the people of this village had come from exchanging women's magazines, and afterwards she had gone on with her reading by herself. She was quite indiscriminate and had little understanding of literature, and she borrowed even the novels and magazines she found lying in the guests' rooms at the inn. Not a few of the new novelists whose names came to her meant nothing to Shimamura. Her manner was as though she were talking of a distant foreign literature. There was something lonely, something sad in it, something that rather suggested a beggar who has lost all desire. It occurred to Shimamura that his own distant fantasy on the occidental ballet, built up from words and photographs in foreign books, was not in its way dissimilar.

She talked on happily too of movies and plays she had never seen. She had no doubt been starved all these months for someone who would listen to her. Had she forgotten that a hundred and ninety-nine days earlier exactly this sort of conversation had set off the impulse to throw herself at Shimamura? Again she lost herself in the talk, and again her words seemed to be warming her whole body.

But her longing for the city had become an undemanding dream, wrapped in simple resignation, and the note of wasted effort was much stronger in it than any suggestion of the exile's lofty dissatisfaction. She did not seem to find herself especially sad, but in Shimamura's eyes there was something strangely touching about her. Were he to give himself quite up to that consciousness of wasted effort, Shimamura felt, he would be drawn into a remote emotionalism that would make his own life a waste. But before him was the quick, live face of the woman, ruddy from the mountain air.

In any case, he had revised his view of her, and he had found, surprisingly, that her being a geisha made it even more difficult for him to be free and open with her.

Dead-drunk that night, she had savagely bitten her half-paralyzed arm in a fit of irritation at its recalcitrance. "What's the matter with you? Damn you, damn you. Lazy, worthless. What's the matter with you?"

And, unable to stand, she had rolled from side to side. "I'll never have any regrets. But I'm not that sort of woman. I'm not that sort of woman."

"The midnight for Tokyo." The woman seemed

to sense his hesitation, and she spoke as if to push it away. At the sound of the train whistle she stood up. Roughly throwing open a paper-paneled door and the window behind it, she sat down on the sill with her body thrown back against the railing. The train moved off into the distance, its echo fading into a sound as of the night wind. Cold air flooded the room.

"Have you lost your mind?" Shimamura too went over to the window. The air was still, without a suggestion of wind.

It was a stern night landscape. The sound of the freezing of snow over the land seemed to roar deep into the earth. There was no moon. The stars, almost too many of them to be true, came forward so brightly that it was as if they were falling with the swiftness of the void. As the stars came nearer, the sky retreated deeper and deeper into the night color. The layers of the Border Range, indistinguishable one from another, cast their heaviness at the skirt of the starry sky in a blackness grave and somber enough to communicate their mass. The whole of the night scene came together in a clear, tranquil harmony.

As she sensed Shimamura's approach, the woman fell over with her breast against the railing. There was no hint of weakness in the pose. Rather, against the night, it was the strongest and most stubborn

she could have taken. So we have to go through
that again, thought Shimamura.

Black though the mountains were, they seemed
at that moment brilliant with the color of the snow.
They seemed to him somehow transparent, somehow lonely. The harmony between sky and mountains was lost.

Shimamura put his hand to the woman's throat.
"You'll catch cold. See how cold it is." He tried to
pull her back, but she clung to the railing.

"I'm going home." Her voice was choked.

"Go home, then."

"Let me stay like this a little longer."

"I'm going down for a bath."

"No, stay here with me."

"If you close the window."

"Let me stay here like this a little longer."

Half the village was hidden behind the cedars of
the shrine grove. The light in the railway station,
not ten minutes away by taxi, flickered on and off
as if crackling in the cold.

The woman's hair, the glass of the window, the
sleeve of his kimono—everything he touched was
cold in a way Shimamura had never known before.

Even the straw mats under his feet seemed cold.
He started down to the bath.

"Wait. I'll go with you." The woman followed
meekly.

As she was rearranging the clothes he had thrown to the floor outside the bath, another guest, a man, came in. The woman crouched low in front of Shimamura and hid her face.

"Excuse me." The other guest started to back away.

"No, please," Shimamura said quickly. "We'll go next door." He scooped up his clothes and stepped over to the women's bath. The woman followed as if they were married. Shimamura plunged into the bath without looking back at her. He felt a high laugh mount to his lips now that he knew she was with him. He put his face to the hot-water tap and noisily rinsed his mouth.

Back in the room, she raised her head a little from the pillow and pushed her side hair up with her little finger.

"This makes me very sad." She said only that. Shimamura thought for a moment that her eyes were half open, but he saw that the thick eyelashes created the illusion.

The woman, always high-strung, did not sleep the whole night.

It was apparently the sound of the *obi* being tied that awakened Shimamura.

"I'm sorry. I should have let you sleep. It's still

dark. Look—can you see me?" She turned off the
light. "Can you see me? You can't?"

"I can't see you. It's still pitch dark."

"No, no. I want you to look close. Now. Can
you see me?" She threw open the window. "It's no
good. You can see me. I'm going."

Surprised anew at the morning cold, Shimamura
raised his head from the pillow. The sky was still
the color of night, but in the mountains it was already morning.

"But it's all right. The farmers aren't busy this
time of the year, and no one will be out so early.
But do you suppose someone might be going out
into the mountains?" She talked on to herself, and
she walked about trailing the end of the half-tied
obi. "There were no guests on the five-o'clock from
Tokyo. None of the inn people will be up for a
long while yet."

Even when she had finished tying the *obi*, she
stood up and sat down and stood up again, and
wandered about the room with her eye on the window. She seemed on edge, like some restless night
beast that fears the approach of the morning. It was
as though a strange, magical wildness had taken her.

Presently the room was so light that he could see
the red of her cheeks. His eye was fastened on that
extraordinarily bright red.

"Your cheeks are flaming. That's how cold it is."

"It's not from the cold. It's because I've taken off my powder. I only have to get into bed and in a minute I'm warm as an oven. All the way to my feet." She knelt at the mirror by the bed.

"It's daylight. I'm going home."

Shimamura glanced up at her, and immediately lowered his head. The white in the depths of the mirror was the snow, and floating in the middle of it were the woman's bright red cheeks. There was an indescribably fresh beauty in the contrast.

Was the sun already up? The brightness of the snow was more intense, it seemed to be burning icily. Against it, the woman's hair became a clearer black, touched with a purple sheen.

Probably to keep snow from piling up, the water from the baths was led around the walls of the inn by a makeshift ditch, and in front of the entrance it spread out like a shallow spring. A powerful black dog stood on the stones by the doorway lapping at the water. Skis for the hotel guests, probably brought out from a storeroom, were lined up to dry, and the faint smell of mildew was sweetened by the steam. The snow that had fallen from the cedar branches to the roof of the public bath was breaking down into something warm and shapeless.

By the end of the year, that road would be shut

off from sight by the snowstorms. She would have to go to her parties in long rubber boots with baggy "mountain trousers" over her kimono, and she would have a cape pulled around her and a veil over her face. The snow would by then be ten feet deep—the woman had looked down on the steep road from the window of the inn, high on a hill, before daybreak this morning, and now Shimamura was walking down the same road. Diapers hung high beside the road to dry. Under them stretched the vista of the Border Range, the snow on its peaks glowing softly. The green onions in the garden patches were not yet buried in the snow.

Children of the village were skiing in the fields.

As he started into the part of the village that fronted on the highway, he heard a sound as of quiet rain.

Little icicles glistened daintily along the eaves.

"While you're at it, would you mind shoveling a little from ours?" Dazzled by the bright light, a woman on her way back from the bath wiped at her forehead with a damp towel as she looked up at a man shoveling snow from a roof. A waitress, probably, who had drifted into the village a little in advance of the skiing season. Next door was a café with a sagging roof, its painted window flaking with age.

Rows of stones held down the shingles with which most of the houses along the street were roofed. Only on the side exposed to the sun did the round stones show their black surfaces, less a moist black from the melting snow than an ink-stone black, beaten away at by icy wind and storm. The houses were of a kind with the dark stones on their roofs. The low eaves hugging the ground seemed to have in them the very essence of the north country.

Children were breaking off chunks of ice from the drains and throwing them down in the middle of the road. It was no doubt the sparkle of the ice as it went flying off into bits that enchanted them so. Shimamura, standing in the sunlight, found it hard to believe that the ice could be so thick. He stopped for a moment to watch.

A girl of twelve or thirteen stood knitting apart from the rest, her back against a stone wall. Under the baggy "mountain trousers," her feet were bare but for sandals, and Shimamura could see that the soles were red and cracked from the cold. A girl of perhaps two stood on a bundle of firewood beside her patiently holding a ball of yarn. Even the faded, ashen line of reclaimed yarn from the younger girl to the older seemed warmly aglow.

He could hear a carpenter's plane in a ski shop seven or eight doors down the street. Five or six geisha were talking under the eaves opposite. Among them, he was sure, would be the woman, Komako—he had just that morning learned her geisha name from a maid at the inn. And indeed, there she was. She had apparently noticed him. The deadly serious expression on her face set her off from the others. She would of course flush scarlet, but if she could at least pretend that nothing had happened—before Shimamura had time to go further with his thoughts, he saw that she had flushed to the throat. She might better have looked away, but her head turned little by little to follow him, while her eyes were fixed on the ground in acute discomfort.

Shimamura's cheeks too were aflame. He walked briskly by, and immediately Komako came after him.

"You mustn't. You embarrass me, walking by at a time like this."

"I embarrass you—you think I'm not embarrassed myself, with all of you lined up to waylay me? I could hardly make myself walk past. Is it always this way?"

"Yes, I suppose so. In the afternoon."

"But I'd think you'd be even more embarrassed, turning bright red and then chasing after me."

"What difference does it make?" The words were clear and definite, but she was blushing again. She stopped and put her arm around a persimmon tree beside the road. "I ran after you because I thought I might ask you to come by my house."

"Is your house near here?"

"Very near."

"I'll come if you'll let me read your diary."

"I'm going to burn my diary before I die."

"But isn't there a sick man in your house?"

"How did you know?"

"You were at the station to meet him yesterday. You had on a dark-blue cape. I was sitting near him on the train. And there was a woman with him, looking after him, as gentle as she could be. His wife? Or someone who went from here to bring him home? Or someone from Tokyo? She was exactly like a mother. I was very much impressed."

"Why didn't you say so last night? Why were you so quiet?" Something had upset her.

"His wife?"

Komako did not answer. "Why didn't you say anything last night? What a strange person you are."

Shimamura did not like this sharpness. Nothing he had done and nothing that had happened seemed to call for it, and he wondered if something basic in the woman's nature might not be coming to the surface. Still, when she came at him

the second time, he had to admit that he was being hit in a vulnerable spot. This morning, as he
glanced at Komako in that mirror reflecting the
mountain snow, he had of course thought of the
girl in the evening train window. Why then had
he said nothing?

"It doesn't matter if there is a sick man. No one
ever comes to my room." Komako went in through
an opening in a low stone wall.

To the right was a small field, and to the left
persimmon trees stood along the wall that marked
off the neighboring plot. There seemed to be a
flower garden in front of the house, and red carp
were swimming in the little lotus pond. The ice
had been broken away and lay piled along the
bank. The house was old and decayed, like the
pitted trunk of a persimmon. There were patches
of snow on the roof, the rafters of which sagged to
draw a wavy line at the eaves.

The air in the earthen-floored hallway was still
and cold. Shimamura was led up a ladder before
his eyes had become accustomed to the darkness.
It was a ladder in the truest sense of the word,
and the room at the top was an attic.

"This is the room the silkworms used to live in.
Are you surprised?"

"You're lucky you've never fallen downstairs,
drinking the way you do."

"I have. But generally when I've had too much to drink I crawl into the *kotatsu* downstairs and go off to sleep." She pushed her hand tentatively into the *kotatsu*, then went below for charcoal. Shimamura looked around at the curious room. Although there was but one low window, opening to the south, the freshly changed paper on the door turned off the rays of the sun brightly. The walls had been industriously pasted over with rice paper, so that the effect was rather like the inside of an old-fashioned paper box; but overhead was only the bare roof sloping down toward the window, as if a dark loneliness had settled itself over the room. Wondering what might be on the other side of the wall, Shimamura had the uneasy feeling that he was suspended in a void. But the walls and the floor, for all their shabbiness, were spotlessly clean.

For a moment he was taken with the fancy that the light must pass through Komako, living in the silkworms' room, as it passed through the translucent silkworms.

The *kotatsu* was covered with a quilt of the same rough, striped cotton material as the standard "mountain trousers." The chest of drawers was old, but the grain of the wood was fine and straight—perhaps it was a relic of Komako's years in Tokyo. It was badly paired with a cheap dresser,

while the vermilion sewing-box gave off the luxuri-
ous glow of good lacquer. The boxes stacked along
the wall behind a thin woolen curtain apparently
served as bookshelves.

The kimono of the evening before hung on the
wall, open to show the brilliant red under-kimono.

Komako came spryly up the ladder with a sup-
ply of charcoal.

"It's from the sickroom. But you needn't worry.
They say fire spreads no germs." Her newly
dressed hair almost brushed the *kotatsu* as she
stirred away at the coals. The music teacher's son
had intestinal tuberculosis, she said, and had come
home to die.

But it was not entirely accurate to say that he
had "come home." He had as a matter of fact not
been born here. This was his mother's home. His
mother had taught dancing down on the coast even
when she was no longer a geisha, but she had had a
stroke while she was still in her forties, and had
come back to this hot spring to recover. The son,
fond of machinery since he was a child, had stayed
behind to work in a watch-shop. Presently he
moved to Tokyo and started going to night school,
and the strain was evidently too much for him. He
was only twenty-five.

All this Komako told him with no hesitation,
but she said nothing about the girl who had

brought the man home, and nothing about why she herself was in this house.

Shimamura felt most uncomfortable at what she did say, however. Suspended there in the void, she seemed to be broadcasting to the four directions.

As he stepped from the hallway, he saw something faintly white through the corner of his eye. It was a samisen box, and it struck him as larger and longer than it should be. He found it hard to imagine her carrying so unwieldy an object to parties. The darkened door inside the hallway slid open.

"Do you mind if I step over this, Komako?" It was that clear voice, so beautiful that it was almost sad. Shimamura waited for an echo to come back.

It was Yoko's voice, the voice that had called out over the snow to the station master the night before.

"No, please go ahead." Yoko stepped lightly over the samisen box, a glass chamber-pot in her hand.

It was clear, from the familiar way she had talked to the station master the evening before and from the way she wore "mountain trousers," that she was a native of this snow country, but the bold pattern of her *obi*, half visible over the trousers, made the rough russet and black stripes of the latter seem fresh and cheerful, and for the same reason the long sleeves of her woolen kimono took on a certain voluptuous charm. The trousers, split just below the knees, filled out toward the hips, and the heavy cotton, for all its natural stiffness, was somehow supple and gentle.

Yoko darted one quick, piercing glance at Shimamura and went silently out over the earthen floor.

Even when he had left the house, Shimamura was haunted by that glance, burning just in front of his forehead. It was cold as a very distant light, for the inexpressible beauty of it had made his heart rise when, the night before, that light off in the mountains had passed across the girl's face in the train window and lighted her eye for a moment. The impression came back to Shimamura, and with it the memory of the mirror filled with snow, and Komako's red cheeks floating in the middle of it.

He walked faster. His legs were round and plump, but he was seized with a certain abandon as he walked along gazing at the mountains he was so fond of, and his pace quickened, though he hardly knew it. Always ready to give himself up to reverie, he could not believe that the mirror floating over the evening scenery and the other snowy mirror were really works of man. They were part of nature, and part of some distant world.

And the room he had only this moment left had become part of that same distant world.

Startled at himself, in need of something to cling to, he stopped a blind masseuse at the top of the hill.

"Could you give me a massage?"

"Let me see. What time will it be?" She tucked her cane under her arm and, taking a covered pocket watch from her *obi*, felt at the face with her left hand. "Two thirty-five. I have an appointment over beyond the station at three-thirty. But I suppose it won't matter if I'm a little late."

"You're very clever to be able to tell the time."

"It has no glass, and I can feel the hands."

"You can feel the figures?"

"Not the figures." She took the watch out again, a silver one, large for a woman, and flicked open the lid. She laid her fingers across the face with one at twelve and one at six, and a third halfway between at three. "I can tell the time fairly well. I may be a minute off one way or the other, but I never miss by as much as two minutes."

"You don't find the road a little slippery?"

"When it rains my daughter comes to call for me. At night I take care of the people in the village, and never come up this far. The maids at the inn are always joking and saying its because my husband won't let me go out at night."

"Your children are growing up?"

"The oldest girl is twelve." They had reached Shimamura's room, and they were silent for a time as the massaging began. The sound of a samisen came to them from the distance.

"Who would that be, I wonder."

"You can always tell which geisha it is by the tone?"

"I can tell some of them. Some I can't. You must not have to work. Feel how nice and soft you are."

"No stiff muscles on me."

"A little stiff here at the base of the neck. But you're just right, not too fat and not too thin. And you don't drink, do you?"

"You can tell that?"

"I have three other customers with physiques exactly like yours."

"A common sort of physique."

"But when you don't drink, you don't know what it is really to enjoy yourself—to forget everything that happens."

"Your husband drinks, does he?"

"Much too much."

"But whoever it is, she's not much of a musician."

"Very poor indeed."

"Do you play yourself?"

"I did when I was young. From the time I was

eight till I was nineteen. I haven't played in fifteen years now. Not since I was married."

Did all blind people look younger than they were? Shimamura wondered.

"But if you learn when you're young, you never forget."

"My hands have changed from doing this sort of work, but my ear is still good. It makes me very impatient to hear them playing. But then I suppose I felt impatient at my own playing when I was young." She listened for a time. "Fumi at the Izutsuya, maybe. The best ones and the worst are the easiest to tell."

"There are good ones?"

"Komako is very good. She's young, but she's improved a great deal lately."

"Really?"

"You know her, don't you? I say she's good, but you have to remember that our standards here in the mountains are not very high."

"I don't really know her. I was on the train with the music teacher's son last night, though."

"He's well again?"

"Apparently not."

"Oh? He's been sick for a long time in Tokyo, and they say it was to help pay the doctors' bills that Komako became a geisha last summer. I wonder if it did any good."

"Komako, you say?"

"They were only engaged. But I suppose you feel better afterwards if you've done everything you can."

"She was engaged to him?"

"So they say. I don't really know, but that's the rumor."

It was almost too ordinary a thing to hear gossip about geisha from the hot-spring masseuse, and that fact had the perverse effect of making the news the more startling; and Komako's having become a geisha to help her fiancé was so ordinary a bit of melodrama that he found himself almost refusing to accept it. Perhaps certain moral considerations—questions of the propriety of selling oneself as a geisha—helped the refusal.

Shimamura was beginning to think he would like to go deeper into the story, but the masseuse was silent.

If Komako was the man's fiancée, and Yoko was his new lover, and the man was going to die—the expression "wasted effort" again came into Shimamura's mind. For Komako thus to guard her promise to the end, for her even to sell herself to pay doctors' bills—what was it if not wasted effort?

He would accost her with this fact, he would drive it home, when he saw her again, he said to himself; and yet her existence seemed to have become purer and cleaner for this new bit of knowledge.

Aware of a shameful danger lurking in his numbed sense of the false and empty, he lay concentrating on it, trying to feel it, for some time after the masseuse left. He was chilled to the pit of his stomach—but someone had left the windows wide open.

The color of evening had already fallen on the mountain valley, early buried in shadows. Out of the dusk the distant mountains, still reflecting the light of the evening sun, seemed to have come much nearer.

Presently, as the mountain chasms were far and near, high and low, the shadows in them began to deepen, and the sky was red over the snowy mountains, bathed now in but a wan light.

Cedar groves stood out darkly by the river bank, at the ski ground, around the shrine.

Like a warm light, Komako poured in on the empty wretchedness that had assailed Shimamura.

There was a meeting at the inn to discuss plans for the ski season. She had been called in for the party afterwards. She put her hands into the *kotatsu*, then quickly reached up and stroked Shimamura's cheek.

"You're pale this evening. Very strange." She clutched at the soft flesh of his cheek as if to tear it away. "Aren't you the foolish one, though."

She already seemed a little drunk. When she came back from the party she collapsed before the mirror, and drunkenness came out on her face to almost comic effect. "I know nothing about it. Nothing. My head aches. I feel terrible. Terrible. I want a drink. Give me water."

She pressed both hands to her face and tumbled over with little concern for her carefully dressed hair. Presently she brought herself up again and began cleaning away the thick powder with cold cream. The face underneath was a brilliant red. She was quite delighted with herself. To Shimamura it was astonishing that drunkenness could pass so quickly. Her shoulders were shaking from the cold.

All through August she had been near nervous collapse, she told him quietly.

"I thought I'd go mad. I kept brooding over something, and I didn't know myself what it was. It was terrifying. I couldn't sleep. I kept myself under control only when I went out to a party. I had all sorts of dreams, and I lost my appetite. I would sit there jabbing at the floor for hours on end, all through the hottest part of the day."

"When did you first go out as a geisha?"

"In June. I thought for a while I might go to Hamamatsu."

"Get married?"

She nodded. The man had been after her to marry him, but she couldn't like him. She had had great trouble deciding what to do.

"But if you didn't like him, what were you so undecided about?"

"It's not that simple."

"Marriage has so much charm?"

"Don't be nasty. It's more that I want to have everything around me tidy and in order."

Shimamura grunted.

"You're not a very satisfying person, you know."

"Was there something between you and the man from Hamamatsu?"

She flung out her answer: "If there had been, do you think I would have hesitated? But he said that as long as I stayed here, he wouldn't let me marry anyone else. He said he would do everything possible to stand in the way."

"But what could he do from as far away as Hamamatsu? You worried about that?"

Komako stretched out for a time, enjoying the warmth of her body. When she spoke again, her tone was quite casual. "I thought I was pregnant." She giggled. "It seems ridiculous when I look back on it now."

She curled up like a little child, and grabbed at the neck of his kimono with her two fists.

The rich eyelashes again made him think that her eyes were half open.

Her elbow against the brazier, Komako was scribbling something on the back of an old magazine when Shimamura awoke the next morning.

"I can't go home. I jumped up when the maid came to bring charcoal, but it was already broad daylight. The sun was shining in on the door. I was a little drunk last night, and I slept too well."

"What time is it?"

"It's already eight."

"Let's go have a bath." Shimamura got out of bed.

"I can't. Someone might see me in the hall." She was completely tamed. When Shimamura came back from the bath, he found her industriously cleaning the room, a kerchief draped artistically over her head.

She had polished the legs of the table and the edge of the brazier almost too carefully, and she stirred up the charcoal with a practiced hand.

Shimamura sat idly smoking, his feet in the *kotatsu*. When the ashes dropped from his cigarette Komako took them up in a handkerchief and brought him an ashtray. He laughed, a bright morning laugh. Komako laughed too.

"If you had a husband, you'd spend all your time scolding him."

❦

"I would not. But I'd be laughed at for folding up even my dirty clothes. I can't help it. That's the way I am."

"They say you can tell everything about a woman by looking inside her dresser drawers."

"What a beautiful day." They were having breakfast, and the morning sun flooded the room. "I should have gone home early to practice the samisen. The sound is different on a day like this." She looked up at the crystal-clear sky.

The snow on the distant mountains was soft and creamy, as if veiled in a faint smoke.

Shimamura, remembering what the masseuse had said, suggested that she practice here instead. Immediately she telephoned her house to ask for music and a change of clothes.

So the house he had seen the day before had a telephone, thought Shimamura. The eyes of the other girl, Yoko, floated into his mind.

"That girl will bring your music?"

"She might."

"You're engaged to the son, are you?"

"Well! When did you hear that?"

"Yesterday."

"Aren't you strange? If you heard it yesterday, why didn't you tell me?" But her tone showed none of the sharpness of the day before. Today there was only a clean smile on her face.

"That sort of thing would be easier to talk about if I had less respect for you."

"What are you really thinking, I wonder? That's why I don't like Tokyo people."

"You're trying to change the subject. You haven't answered my question, you know."

"I'm not trying to change the subject. You really believed it?"

"I did."

"You're lying again. You didn't really."

"I couldn't quite believe all of it, as a matter of fact. But they said you went to work as a geisha to help pay doctors' bills."

"It sounds like something out of a cheap magazine. But it's not true. I was never engaged to him. People seem to think I was, though. It wasn't to help anyone in particular that I became a geisha. But I owe a great deal to his mother, and I had to do what I could."

"You're talking in riddles."

"I'll tell you everything. Very clearly. There does seem to have been a time when his mother thought it would be a good idea for us to get married. But she only thought it. She never said a word. Both of us knew in a vague sort of way what was on her mind, but it went no farther. And that's all there is to tell."

"Childhood friends."

🌷

"That's right. But we've lived most of our lives apart. When they sent me to Tokyo to be a geisha, he was the only one who saw me off. I have that written down on the very first page of my very oldest diary."

"If the two of you had stayed together, you'd probably be married by now."

"I doubt it."

"You would be, though."

"You needn't worry about him. He'll be dead before long."

"But is it right for you to be spending your nights away from home?"

"It's not right for you to ask. How can a dying man keep me from doing as I like?"

Shimamura could think of no answer.

Why was it that Komako said not a word about the girl Yoko?

And Yoko, who had taken care of the sick man on the train, quite as his mother must have when he was very young—how would she feel coming to an inn with a change of kimono for Komako, who was something, Shimamura could not know what, to the man Yoko had come home with?

Shimamura found himself off in his usual distant fantasies.

"Komako, Komako." Yoko's beautiful voice was low but clear.

"Thank you very much." Komako went out to the dressing-room. "You brought it yourself, did you? It must have been heavy."

Yoko left immediately.

The top string snapped as Komako plucked tentatively at the samisen. Shimamura could tell even while she was changing the string and tuning the instrument that she had a firm, confident touch. She took up a bulky bundle and undid it on the *kotatsu*. Inside were an ordinary book of lyrics and some twenty scores. Shimamura glanced curiously at the latter.

"You practice from these?"

"I have to. There's no one here who can teach me."

"What about the woman you live with?"

"She's paralyzed."

"If she can talk she ought to be able to help you."

"But she can't talk. She can still use her left hand to correct mistakes in dancing, but it only annoys her to have to listen to the samisen and not be able to do anything about it."

"Can you really understand the music from only a score?"

"I understand it very well."

"The publishing gentleman would be happy if he knew he had a real geisha—not just an ordinary amateur—practicing from his scores way off here in the mountains."

"In Tokyo I was expected to dance, and they gave me dancing lessons. But I got only the faintest idea of how to play the samisen. If I were to lose that there would be no one here to teach me again. So I use scores."

"And singing?"

"I don't like to sing. I did learn a few songs from my dancing, and I manage to get through them, but newer things I've had to pick up from the radio. I've no idea how near right I am. My own private style—you'd laugh at it, I know. And then my voice gives out when I'm singing for someone I know well. It's always loud and brave for strangers." She looked a little bashful for a moment, then brought herself up and glanced at Shimamura as though signaling that she was ready for him to begin.

He was embarrassed. He was unfortunately no singer.

He was generally familiar with the Nagauta music of the Tokyo theater and dance, and he knew the words to most of the repertoire. He had had no formal training, however. Indeed he associated the Nagauta less with the parlor performance of the geisha than with the actor on the stage.

"The customer is being difficult." Giving her lower lip a quick little bite, Komako brought the samisen to her knee, and, as if that made her a different person, turned earnestly to the lyrics before her.

"I've been practicing this one since last fall."

A chill swept over Shimamura. The goose flesh seemed to rise even to his cheeks. The first notes opened a transparent emptiness deep in his entrails, and in the emptiness the sound of the samisen reverberated. He was startled—or, better, he fell back as under a well-aimed blow. Taken with a feeling almost of reverence, washed by waves of remorse, defenseless, quite deprived of strength—there was nothing for him to do but give himself up to the current, to the pleasure of being swept off wherever Komako would take him.

She was a mountain geisha, not yet twenty, and she could hardly be as good as all that, he told himself. And in spite of the fact that she was in a small room, was she not slamming away at the instrument as though she were on the stage? He was being carried away by his own mountain emotionalism. Komako purposely read the words in a monotone, now slowing down and now jumping over a passage that was too much trouble; but gradually she seemed to fall into a spell. As her voice rose higher, Shimamura began to feel a little frightened. How far would that strong, sure touch take him? He rolled over and pillowed his head on an arm, as if in bored indifference.

The end of the song released him. Ah, this woman is in love with me—but he was annoyed with himself for the thought.

Komako looked up at the clear sky over the snow. "The tone is different on a day like this." The tone had been as rich and vibrant as her remark suggested. The air was different. There were no theater walls, there was no audience, there was none of the city dust. The notes went out crystalline into the clean winter morning, to sound on the far, snowy peaks.

Practicing alone, not aware herself of what was happening, perhaps, but with all the wideness of nature in this mountain valley for her companion, she had come quite as a part of nature to take on this special power. Her very loneliness beat down sorrow and fostered a wild strength of will. There was no doubt that it had been a great victory of the will, even granted that she had had an amount of preparatory training, for her to learn complicated airs from only a score, and presently go through them from memory.

To Shimamura it was wasted effort, this way of living. He sensed in it too a longing that called out to him for sympathy. But the life and way of living no doubt flowed thus grandly from the samisen with a new worth for Komako herself.

Shimamura, untrained in the niceties of samisen technique and conscious only of the emotion in the tone, was perhaps an ideal audience for Komako.

By the time she had begun her third song—the voluptuous softness of the music itself may have been responsible—the chill and the goose flesh had disappeared, and Shimamura, relaxed and warm, was gazing into Komako's face. A feeling of intense physical nearness came over him.

The high, thin nose was usually a little lonely, a little sad, but today, with the healthy, vital flush on her cheeks, it was rather whispering: I am here too. The smooth lips seemed to reflect back a dancing light even when they were drawn into a tight bud; and when for a moment they were stretched wide, as the singing demanded, they were quick to contract again into that engaging little bud. Their charm was exactly like the charm of her body itself. Her eyes, moist and shining, made her look like a very young girl. She wore no powder, and the polish of the city geisha had over it a layer of mountain color. Her skin, suggesting the newness of a freshly peeled onion or perhaps a lily bulb, was flushed faintly, even to the throat. More than anything, it was clean.

Seated rigidly upright, she seemed more demure and maidenly than usual.

This time using a score, she sang a song she had not yet finished memorizing. At the end she silently pushed the plectrum under the strings and let herself fall into an easier posture.

Her manner quickly took on a touch of the seductive and alluring.

Shimamura could think of nothing to say. Komako did not seem to care particularly what he thought of her playing, however. She was quite unaffectedly pleased with herself.

"Can you always tell which geisha it is from the tone of the samisen?"

"That's easy. There aren't twenty of us all together. It depends a little on the style, though. The individual comes out more in some styles than in others."

She took up the samisen again and shifted her weight so that her feet were a little to one side and the instrument rested on the calf of one leg.

"This is the way you hold it when you're small." She leaned toward the samisen as though it were too large for her. "Da-a-ark hair. . . ." Her voice was deliberately childish and she picked out the notes uncertainly.

" 'Dark Hair' was the first one you learned?"

"Uh-uh." She shook her head girlishly, as no

doubt she did in the days when she was still too small to hold the samisen properly.

Komako no longer tried to leave before daybreak when she stayed the night.

"Komako," the two-year-old daughter of the innkeeper would call from far down the hall, her voice rising in the mountain-country lilt. The two of them would play happily in the *kotatsu* until nearly noon, when they would go for a bath.

Back from the bath, Komako was combing her hair. "Whenever the child sees a geisha, she calls out 'Komako' in that funny accent, and when she sees a picture of someone with her hair done in the old way, that's 'Komako' too. Children can tell when you like them. Come, Kimi. Let's go play at Komako's." She stood up to leave, then sat down lazily on the veranda. "Eager people from Tokyo already out skiing."

The room looked from high ground directly south over the ski runs at the base of the mountain.

Shimamura glanced up from the *kotatsu*. There were patches of snow on the mountain, and five or six figures in black ski clothes were moving about in the terraced fields. It seemed a trifle silly. The slope was a gentle one, and the walls between the fields were not yet covered with snow.

"They look like students. Is today Sunday? Do you suppose that's fun?"

"They're good, though," Komako said, as if to herself. "Guests are always surprised when a geisha says hello to them on the ski grounds. They don't recognize her for the snow-burn. At night the powder hides it."

"You wear ski clothes?"

She wore "mountain trousers," she said. "But what a nuisance the ski season is. It's all coming again. You see them in the evening at the inn, and they say they'll see you again the next day skiing. Maybe I should give up skiing this year. Good-by. Come along, Kimi. We'll have snow this evening. It's always cold the night before it snows."

Shimamura went out to the veranda. Komako was leading Kimi down the steep road below the ski grounds.

The sky was clouding over. Mountains still in the sunlight stood out against shadowed mountains. The play of light and shade changed from moment to moment, sketching a chilly landscape. Presently the ski grounds too were in shadow. Below the window Shimamura could see little needles of frost like ising-glass among the withered chrysanthemums, though water was still dripping from the snow on the roof.

It did not snow that evening. A hailstorm turned to rain.

Shimamura called Komako again the night before he was to leave. It was a clear, moonlit night. At eleven o'clock the air was bitterly cold, but Komako insisted on going for a walk. She pulled him roughly from the *kotatsu*.

The road was frozen. The village lay quiet under the cold sky. Komako hitched up the skirt of her kimono and tucked it into her *obi*. The moon shone like a blade frozen in blue ice.

"We'll go to the station," said Komako.

"You're insane. It's more than a mile each way."

"You'll be going back to Tokyo soon. We'll go look at the station."

Shimamura was numb from his shoulders to his thighs.

Back in his room, Komako sank disconsolately to the floor. Her head was bowed and her arms were deep in the *kotatsu*. Strangely, she refused to go with him to the bath.

Bedding had been laid out with the foot of the mattress inside the *kotatsu*. Komako was sitting forlornly beside it when Shimamura came back from the bath. She said nothing.

"What's the matter?"

"I'm going home."

"Don't be foolish."

❦

"Go on to bed. Just let me sit here for a little while."

"Why do you want to go home?"

"I'm not going home. I'll sit here till morning."

"Don't be difficult."

"I'm not being difficult. I'm not being difficult."

"Then . . . ?"

"I . . . don't feel well."

"Is that all?" Shimamura laughed. "I'll leave you quite to yourself."

"No."

"And why did you have to go out and run all over town?"

"I'm going home."

"There's no need to go home."

"But it's not easy for me. Go on back to Tokyo. It's no easy for me." Her face was low over the *kotatsu*.

Was it sorrow at finding herself about to sink into too deep a relationship with a traveler? Or at having to keep herself under control at so dear a moment? She has come that far, then, Shimamura said to himself. He too was silent for a time.

"Please go back to Tokyo."

"As a matter of fact, I was thinking of going back tomorrow."

"No! Why are you going back?" She looked up, startled, as though aroused from sleep.

"What can I do for you, no matter how long I stay?"

She gazed at him for a moment, then burst out violently: "You don't have to say that. What reason have you to say that?" She stood up irritably, and threw herself at his neck. "It's wrong of you to say such things. Get up. Get up, I tell you." The words poured out deliriously, and she fell down beside him, quite forgetting in her derangement the physical difficulty she had spoken of earlier.

Some time later, she opened warm, moist eyes.

She picked up the hair ornament that had fallen to the floor.

"You really must go back tomorrow," she said quietly.

As Shimamura was changing clothes to leave on the three-o'clock train the next afternoon, the manager of the inn beckoned Komako into the hall. "Let's see. Suppose we make it about eleven hours," he could hear Komako's answer. They were evidently discussing the bill for her services as a geisha, and the manager perhaps thought it would be unreasonable to charge for the whole sixteen or seventeen hours.

The bill as a matter of fact was computed by the hour—"Left at five," or "Left at twelve"—without the usual charge for overnight services.

Komako, in an overcoat and a white scarf, saw him to the station.

Even when he had finished buying presents to take back to Tokyo, he had some twenty minutes to kill. Walking with Komako in the slightly raised station plaza, he thought what a narrow little valley it was, crowded in among the snowy mountains. Komako's too-black hair was a little touching, a little sad, in the loneliness of the shadowed mountain pocket.

The sun shone dimly on a spot in the mountains far down the river.

"It's melted a good deal since I came."

"Two days of snow, though, and we'll have six feet. Then it snows again, and before long the lights on those poles are out of sight. I'll walk along thinking of you, and I'll find myself strung up on a wire."

"The snow is that deep?"

"They say that in the next town up the line the schoolchildren jump naked from the second floor of the dormitory. They sink out of sight in the snow, and they move around under it as though they were swimming. Look, a snowplow."

"I'd like to see it that deep. But I suppose the inn will be crowded. And there might be danger of slides along the way."

"With you it's not a question of money, is it?

Have you always had so much to spend?" She turned to look up at his face. "Why don't you grow a mustache?"

"I've thought of it." Shimamura, freshly shaven, stroked the blue-black traces of his beard. A deep line from the corner of his mouth set off the softness of his cheek. Was that, he wondered, what Komako found attractive? "You always look a little as though you'd just shaved too when you take off that powder."

"Listen! The crows. That frightening way they sometimes have. Where are they, I wonder? And isn't it cold!" Komako hugged herself as she looked up at the sky.

"Shall we go in by the stove?"

A figure in "mountain trousers" came running up the wide road from the main highway into the station plaza. It was Yoko.

"Komako. Yukio— Komako," she panted, clinging to Komako like a child that has run frightened to its mother, "come home. Right away. Yukio's worse. Right away."

Komako closed her eyes, as if from the pain of the assault on her shoulder. Her face was white, but she shook her head with surprising firmness.

"I can't go home. I'm seeing off a guest."

Shimamura was startled. "You needn't see me off."

"It's not right to leave. How do I know you'll come again?"

"I'll come, I'll come."

Yoko seemed not to hear the exchange. "I just called the inn," she went on feverishly, "and they said you were at the station. So I came here. I ran all the way. Yukio is asking for you." She pulled at Komako, but Komako shook her off impatiently.

"Leave me alone."

It was Komako who reeled back, however. She retched violently, but nothing came from her mouth. The rims of her eyes were moist. There was goose flesh on her checks.

Yoko stood rigid, gazing at Komako. Her face, like a mask, wore an expression of such utter earnestness that it was impossible to tell whether she was angry or surprised or grieved. It seemed an extraordinarily pure and simple face to Shimamura.

She turned quickly and, without the slightest change of expression, clutched at Shimamura's hand. "I'm sorry, but would you let her go home?" A tense, high-pitched voice assailed him. "Let her go home."

"Of course I'll let her go home. Go on home," he called out to Komako. "Don't be a fool."

"And what say do you have in the matter?" Komako pushed Yoko roughly away from him.

Shimamura tried to signal the taxi waiting in front of the station. Yoko clutched at his arm so tightly that his fingers were numbed. "I'll send her home in a taxi," he said. "Why don't you go on ahead? People will be watching us."

Yoko nodded quickly, and turned away with almost unbelievable alacrity. Why was the girl always so earnest, so sober, Shimamura wondered. But such musings did not seem entirely in keeping with the occasion.

That voice, so beautiful it was almost lonely, lingered in Shimamura's ears as if it were echoing back from somewhere in the snowy mountains.

"Where are you going?" Komako pulled at Shimamura. He had signaled the taxi and was walking toward it. "I won't. I'm not going home."

For an instant Shimamura felt something very near physical revulsion.

"I don't know what there is among the three of you, but the man may be dying even now. She came for you, didn't she, because he wants to see you. Go home like a good girl. You'll regret it all your life if you don't. What if he dies even while you're standing here? Don't be stubborn. Forgive and forget."

"Forgive and forget? You don't understand. You don't understand at all."

"And when they sent you to Tokyo, he was the

only one who saw you off, didn't you say? Do you think it's right not to say good-by to the man you yourself said was on the very first page of the very first volume of your diary? This is the very last page of his."

"But I don't want to. I don't want to see a man die."

It could have been the coldest heartlessness or too warm a passion—Shimamura did not know which.

"I'll not be able to write in my diary any more. I'll burn it," she said softly, almost to herself. Her cheeks were flushed. "You're a good, simple person at heart, aren't you? If you really are, I won't mind sending my whole diary to you. You won't laugh at me? You're a good, honest person at heart, I'm sure."

Shimamura was moved by a wave of feeling he could not define himself. He thought he must indeed be the plainest, most honest person in the world. He no longer worried about sending Komako home. She said nothing more.

A porter from the inn came to tell them that the gate to the tracks was open.

Four or five villagers in somber winter dress got on and off the train.

"I'll not go to the platform with you. Good-by." Komako stood inside the closed window of the waiting-room. From the train window it was as though one strange piece of fruit had been left behind in the grimy glass case of a shabby mountain grocery.

The window of the waiting-room was clear for an instant as the train started to move. Komako's face glowed forth, and as quickly disappeared. It was the bright red it had been in the mirror that snowy morning, and for Shimamura that color again seemed to be the point at which he parted with reality.

The train climbed the north slope of the Border Range into the long tunnel. On the far side it moved down a mountain valley. The color of evening was descending from chasms between the peaks. The dim brightness of the winter afternoon seemed to have been sucked into the earth, and the battered old train had shed its bright shell in the tunnel. There was no snow on the south slope.

Following a stream, the train came out on the plain. A mountain, cut at the top in curious notches and spires, fell off in a graceful sweep to the far skirts. Over it the moon was rising. The solid, integral shape of the mountain, taking up the whole of the evening landscape there at the end of the plain, was set off in a deep purple against the pale light of the sky. The moon was no longer an afternoon white, but, faintly colored, it had not yet taken on the clear coldness of the winter night. There was not a bird in the sky. Nothing broke the lines of the wide skirts to the right and the left. Where the mountain swept down to meet the river, a stark white building, a hydroelectric plant perhaps, stood out sharply from the withered scene the train window framed, one last spot saved from the night.

The window began to steam over. The landscape outside was dusky, and the figures of the passengers floated up half-transparent. It was the play of that evening mirror again. The train, probably no more than three or four worn-out, faded, old-fashioned coaches strung together, was not from the same world as the trains one finds on the main lines. The light inside was dim.

Shimamura abandoned himself to the fancy that he had stepped into some unreal conveyance, that he was being borne away in emptiness, cut off from time and place. The monotonous sound of the wheels became the woman's voice.

Her words, though short and broken, were a sign that she was alive in all her vital intensity, and he knew he had not forgotten her from the fact that listening was a trial. But to the Shimamura of that moment, moving away from the woman, the voice was already a distant one that could do no more than sharpen the poignancy of travel.

Would Yukio be breathing his last even now? Komako had for reasons of her own refused to go home; and had she then failed to reach his bedside in time?

There were so few passengers that Shimamura felt a little uneasy.

Besides Shimamura himself, there were only a man, probably in his fifties, and opposite him a red-faced girl. A black shawl was thrown over the full flesh of her shoulders, and her cheeks were a wonderful, fiery red. She leaned slightly forward to catch every word the man said, and she answered him happily. A pair off on a long journey together, Shimamura concluded.

As the train pulled into a station behind which rose the chimneys of spinning-factories, however, the man hastily got up, took a wicker trunk from the baggage rack, and threw it out the window to the platform. "Maybe we'll meet again sometime," he called back to the girl as he hurried from the train.

Shimamura suddenly wanted to weep. He had been caught quite off guard, and it struck him afresh that he had said good-by to the woman and was on his way home.

He had not considered the possibility that the two had simply met on the train. The man was perhaps a traveling salesman.

PART TWO

I⊤ was the egg-laying season for moths, Shimamura's wife told him as he left Tokyo, and he was not to leave his clothes hanging in the open. There were indeed moths at the inn. Five or six large corn-colored moths clung to the decorative lantern under the eaves, and in the little dressing-room was a moth whose body was large out of all proportion to its wings.

The windows were still screened from the summer. A moth so still that it might have been glued there clung to one of the screens. Its feelers stood

out like delicate wool, the color of cedar bark, and
its wings, the length of a woman's finger, were a
pale, almost diaphanous green. The ranges of
mountains beyond were already autumn-red in the
evening sun. That one spot of pale green struck
him as oddly like the color of death. The fore and
after wings overlapped to make a deeper green,
and the wings fluttered like thin pieces of paper
in the autumn wind.

Wondering if the moth was alive, Shimamura
went over to the window and rubbed his finger
over the inside of the screen. The moth did not
move. He struck at it with his fist, and it fell like a
leaf from a tree, floating lightly up midway to the
ground.

In front of the cedar grove opposite, dragonflies
were bobbing about in countless swarms, like dan-
delion floss in the wind.

The river seemed to flow from the tips of the
cedar branches.

He thought he would never tire of looking at
the autumn flowers that spread a blanket of silver
up the side of the mountain.

A White-Russian woman, a peddler, was sitting
in the hallway when he came out of the bath. So
you find them even in these mountains— He went
for a closer look.

She appeared to be in her forties. Her face was

wrinkled and dirty, but her skin, where it showed at the full throat and beyond, was a pure, glowing white.

"Where are you from?" Shimamura asked.

"Where am I from? Where am I from?" The woman seemed troubled for an answer. She began to put away her wares, the most ordinary Japanese cosmetics and hair ornaments.

Her skirt, like a dirty sheet wrapped around her, had quite lost the feel of occidental dress, and had taken on instead something of the air of Japan. She carried her wares on her back in a large Japanese-style kerchief. But for all that, she still wore foreign shoes.

The innkeeper's wife stood beside Shimamura watching the Russian leave. The two of them went into the office, where a large woman was seated at the hearth with her back to them. She took her long skirts in her hand as she stood up to go. Her cloak was a formal black.

She was a geisha Shimamura remembered having seen with Komako in an advertising photograph, the two of them on skis with cotton "mountain trousers" pulled over party kimonos. She seemed to be well along in years, plump and to all appearances good-natured.

The innkeeper was warming thick, oblong cakes over the embers.

🌷

"Won't you have one?" he asked Shimamura. "You really must have one. The geisha you saw brought them to celebrate the end of her term."

"She's leaving, is she?"

"Yes."

"She looks like a good sort."

"She was very popular. Today she's going the rounds to say good-by."

Shimamura blew on the cake and bit into it. The hard crust, a little sour, gave off a musty smell.

Outside the window, the bright red of ripe persimmons was bathed in the evening sun. It seemed to send out a red glow even to the bamboo of the pothook over the hearth.

"See how long they are." Shimamura looked out in astonishment at the steep path, down which old women were trudging with bundles of autumn grass on their backs. The grass looked to be twice the height of the women, and the tassels were long and powerful.

"It's *kaya* grass."

"*Kaya*, is it?"

"The government railways built a sort of rest-room, I suppose you would call it, for their hot-spring exhibit, and they thatched the teahouse with *kaya* from these mountains. Someone in Tokyo bought it exactly as it was."

"*Kaya*, is it," Shimamura repeated, half to himself. "It's *kaya* then on the mountain? I thought it must be a flower of some sort."

The first thing that had struck Shimamura's eye as he got off the train was that array of silver-white. High up the mountain, the *kaya* spread out silver in the sun, like the autumn sunlight itself pouring over the face of the mountain. Ah, I am here, something in Shimamura called out as he looked up at it.

But the great strands he saw here seemed quite different in nature from the grasses that had so moved him. The large bundles hid the women carrying them, and rustled against the rocks that flanked the path. And the plumes were long and powerful.

Under the dim light in the dressing-room, Shimamura could see that the large-bodied moth was laying eggs along the black lacquer of the clothes-frame. Moths were beating at the lantern under the eaves.

There was a steady humming of autumn insects, as there had been from before sundown.

Komako was a little late.

She gazed in at him from the hall.

"Why have you come here? Why have you come to a place like this?"

"I've come to see you."

"You don't mean that. I dislike people from To-kyo because they're always lying." She sat down, and her voice was softer. "I'm never going to see anyone off again. I can't describe how it felt to see you off."

"This time I'll go without telling you."

"No. I mean I won't go to the station again."

"What happened to him?"

"He died, of course."

"While you were seeing me off?"

"But that's not the reason. I had no idea I could hate so to see someone off."

Shimamura nodded.

"Where were you on the fourteenth of Febru-ary? I was waiting for you. But I'll know better than to believe you next time."

The fourteenth of February was the "bird-chas-ing festival," a children's festival that had in it the spirit of this snow country. For ten days before the festival the children of the village tramped down the snow with straw boots, and presently, cutting the now boardlike snow into two-foot cubes, they built a snow palace some six yards square and more than ten feet high. Since the New Year was celebrated here early in February, the traditional straw ropes were still strung up over the village doorways. On the fourteenth the children gath-ered the ropes and burned them in a red bonfire before the snow palace. They pushed and jostled one another on the roof and sang the bird-chasing song, and afterwards, setting out lights, they spent the night in the palace. At dawn on the fifteenth they again climbed to the roof to sing the bird-chasing song.

It was then that the snow was deepest, and Shimamura had told Komako he would come for the festival.

"I was at home in February. I took a vacation. I was sure you would be here on the fourteenth, and I came back especially. I could have stayed to take care of her longer if I had known."

"Was someone ill?"

"The music teacher. She had pneumonia down on the coast. The telegram came when I was at home, and I went down to take care of her."

"Did she get better?"

"No."

"I'm sorry." Shimamura's words could have been either an expression of sympathy or an apology for the broken promise.

Komako shook her head mildly, and wiped at the table with her handkerchief. "The place is alive with insects." A swarm of tiny winged insects fell from the table to the floor. Several small moths were circling the light.

Moths, how many kinds he could not tell,

dotted the screen, floating on the clear moonlight.

"My stomach aches." Komako thrust both hands tight inside her *obi*, and her head fell to Shimamura's knee. "My stomach aches."

Insects smaller than moths gathered on the thick white powder at her neck. Some of them died there as Shimamura watched.

The flesh on her neck and shoulders was richer than it had been the year before. She is just twenty, he told himself.

He felt something warm and damp on his knee.

" 'Komako, go on up and look in the Camellia Room,' they said in the office, very pleased with themselves. I don't like that way they have. I'd been to see Kikuyu off, and I was just ready for a good nap when someone said there had been a call from here. I didn't feel like coming. I had too much to drink last night at Kikuyu's farewell party. They only laughed down in the office and wouldn't tell me who was here. And it was you. It's been a whole year. You're the sort that comes only once a year?"

"I had one of the cakes she left."

"You did?" Komako sat up. Her face was red where it had been pressed against his knee. She seemed very young.

She had seen the old geisha Kikuyu to the second station down the line, she said.

"It's very sad. We used to be able to work things out together, but now it's every geisha for herself. The place has changed. New geisha come in and no one gets along with anyone else. I'll be lonesome without Kikuyu. She was at the center of everything. And she made more money than any of the rest of us. Her people took very good care of her."

Kikuyu had worked out her contract, and she was going home. Would she get married or would she open an inn or restaurant of her own? Shimamura asked.

"Kikuyu is a very sad case. She made a bad marriage, and she came here afterwards." Komako was silent for a time, evidently unsure how much she should tell. She looked out toward the slope below the terraced fields, bright in the moonlight. "You know the new house halfway up the hill?"

"The restaurant—the Kikumura, is it called?"

"That's the one. Kikuyu was supposed to manage the Kikumura, but at the last minute she had a change of heart. It caused all sorts of excitement. She had a patron build the place for her, and then, when she was all ready to move in, she threw it over. She found someone she liked and was going to marry him, but he ran off and left her. Is that what happens when you lose your head over a man? I wonder. She can't very well go back to her old work, and she can't take over the restaurant now that she's turned it down, and she's ashamed to stay here after all that's happened. There's nothing for her to do but start over somewhere else. It makes me very sad to think about Kikuyu. There were all sorts of people—but of course we don't really know the details."

"Men? How many? Five or so?"

"I wonder." Komako laughed softly and turned away. "Kikuyu was weak. A weakling."

"Maybe there was nothing else she could do."

"But isn't it so? You can't go losing your head over every man that likes you." Her eyes were on the floor, and she was stroking her hair meditatively with a hair ornament. "It wasn't easy, seeing her off."

"And what happened to the restaurant?"

"The wife of the man who built it has taken it over."

"An interesting situation. The wife managing the mistress's restaurant."

"But what else could they do? The place was ready to open, and the wife moved in with all her children."

"What about her own house?"

"They left the old woman to take care of it, I hear. The man's a farmer, but he likes to have his fun. He's a very interesting fellow."

"So it would seem. Is he well along in years?"

"He's young. No more than thirty-one or thirty-two."

"The mistress must be older than the wife, then."

"They're both twenty-six."

"The 'Kiku' of 'Kikumura' would be from 'Kikuyu.' And the wife took over the name even?"

"But they couldn't change the name once it was advertised."

Shimamura straightened the collar of his kimono. Komako got up to close the window.

"Kikuyu knew all about you. She told me today you were here."

"I saw her down in the office when she came to say good-by."

"Did she say anything to you?"

"Not a thing."

"Do you know how I feel?" Komako threw open the window she had just shut, and sat down on the sill as if she meant to throw herself out.

"The stars here are different from the stars in Tokyo," Shimamura said after a time. "They seem to float up from the sky."

"Not tonight, though. The moon is too bright. . . . The snow was dreadful this year."

"I understand there were times when the trains couldn't get through."

"I was almost afraid. The roads weren't open until May, a month later than usual. You know the shop up at the ski grounds? An avalanche went through the second floor of it. The people below heard a strange noise and thought the rats were tearing up the kitchen. There were no rats, though, and when they looked upstairs the place was full of snow and the shutters and all had been carried off. It was just a surface slide, but there was a great deal of talk on the radio. The skiers were frightened away. I said I wouldn't ski any more and I gave my skis away the end of last year, but I went out again after all. Twice, three times maybe. Have I changed?"

"What have you been doing since the music teacher died?"

"Don't you worry about other people's problems. I came back and I was waiting for you in February."

"But if you were down on the coast you could have written me a letter."

"I couldn't. I really couldn't. I couldn't possibly write the sort of letter your wife would see. I couldn't bring myself to. I don't tell lies just because people might be listening." The words came at him in a sudden torrent. He only nodded. "Why don't you turn out the light? You don't have to sit in this swarm of insects."

The moonlight, so bright that the furrows in the woman's ear were clearly shadowed, struck deep into the room and seemed to turn the mats on the floor a chilly green.

"No. Let me go home."

"I see you haven't changed." Shimamura raised his head. There was something strange in her manner. He peered into the slightly aquiline face.

"People say I haven't changed since I came here. I was sixteen then. But life goes on the same, year after year."

Her cheeks still carried the ruddiness of her north-country girlhood. In the moonlight the fine geishalike skin took on the luster of a sea shell.

"But did you hear I'd moved?"

"Since the teacher died? You're not in the silk-worms' room any more, then? This time it's a real geisha house?"

"A real geisha house? I suppose it is. They sell tobacco and candy in the shop, and I'm the only geisha they have. I have a real contract, and when I read late in the night I always use a candle to save electricity."

Shimamura let out a loud guffaw.

"The meter, you know. Shouldn't use too much electricity."

"I see, I see."

"But they're very good to me, so good that I

sometimes find it hard to believe I'm really hired out as a geisha. When one of the children cries, the mother takes it outside so that I won't be bothered. I have nothing to complain about. Only sometimes the bedding is crooked. When I come home late at night, everything is laid out for me, but the mattresses aren't square one on the other, and the sheet is wrong. I hate it. After they've been so kind, though, I feel guilty making the bed over."

"You'd wear yourself out if you had a house of your own."

"So everyone says. There are four little children, and the place is a terrible clutter. I spend the whole day picking things up. I know everything will be thrown down again as soon as my back is turned, but somehow I can't help myself. I want to be as clean and neat as the place will let me. . . . Do you understand how I feel?"

"I understand."

"If you understand, then tell me. Tell me, if you see how I feel." Again that tense, urgent note came into her voice. "See, you can't. Lying again. You have plenty of money, and you're not much of a person. You don't understand at all." She lowered her voice. "I'm very lonely sometimes. But I'm a fool. Go back to Tokyo, tomorrow."

"It's very well for you to condemn me, but how can you expect me to tell you exactly what I mean?"

"Why can't you? It's wrong of you." Her voice was almost desperate. Then she closed her eyes, and began again as if she had asked herself whether Shimamura knew her, felt her for what she was, and had answered that he did. "Once a year is enough. You'll come once a year, won't you, while I'm here?"

Her contract was for four years, she said.

"When I was at home, I didn't dream I would ever be a geisha again. I even gave away my skis before I left. And so all I've accomplished, I suppose, has been to give up smoking."

"I remember how much you used to smoke, now that you mention it."

"When guests at parties give me cigarettes, I tuck them away in my sleeve, and I have a fine collection by the time I'm ready to go home."

"But four years—that's a long time."

"It will pass in a hurry."

"Aren't you warm, though." Shimamura took her in his arms as she came to him.

"I've always been warm."

"I suppose the nights will be getting chilly."

"It's five years now since I came here. At first I

wondered how I could live in such a place—especially before the railroad came through. And it's going on two years since you first came."

He had come three times in less than two years, and on each new visit he had found Komako's life changed.

Crickets were chirping outside in a noisy chorus.

"I wish they'd be a little quieter." Komako pulled away from Shimamura.

The moths at the window started up as the wind came from the north.

Shimamura knew well enough that the thick eyelashes made her eyes seem half open, and yet he found himself looking again to be sure.

"I'm fatter now that I've stopped smoking."

The fat on her abdomen was heavier, he had noticed.

They had long been apart, but what eluded his grasp when he was away from her was immediately near and familiar when he was beside her again.

"One is bigger than the other." She cupped her breasts lightly in her hands.

"I suppose that's a habit of his—one side only."

"What a nasty thing to say!" Here she was—this was it, he remembered.

"Next time tell him to treat them both alike."

"Alike? Shall I tell him to treat them both

alike?" She brought her face gently toward his.

It was a second-floor room, but it seemed to be surrounded by croaking toads. Two and three of them were moving from spot to spot, remarkably long-winded croakers.

Back from the bath, Komako began talking of herself. Her voice was quiet and her manner was completely serene.

The first physical examination she had had here —she thought it would be as when she was an apprentice geisha, and she bared her chest for a tuberculosis check. The doctor laughed, and she burst into tears—such were the intimate details she went into. She talked on as Shimamura encouraged her with questions.

"I'm always exactly on the calendar. Two days less than a month each time."

"I don't suppose it keeps you from your parties?"

"You understand such things, do you?"

Every day she had a bath in the hot spring, famous for its lingering warmth. She walked two miles and more between parties at the old spring and the new, and here in the mountains there were few parties that kept her up late. She was therefore healthy and full-bodied, though she did have a suggestion of the low, bunched-up hips so common with geisha, narrow from side to side and wide from front to back. To Shimamura there was something touching about the fact that such a woman could call him back from afar.

"I wonder if I can have children." And she wondered too if being generally faithful to one man was not the same thing as being married.

That was the first Shimamura had heard of the "one man" in Komako's life. She had known him since she was sixteen, she said. Shimamura thought he understood now the lack of caution that had at first so puzzled him.

She had never liked the man, Komako continued, and had never felt near him, perhaps because the affair had begun when she was down on the coast just after the death of the man who had paid her debts.

"But it's certainly better than average if it's lasted five years."

"I've had two chances to leave him. When I went to work as a geisha here, and when I moved after the music teacher died. But I've never had the will power to do it. I don't have much will power."

The man was still down on the coast. It had not been convenient to keep her there, and when the music teacher came back to these mountains he had left Komako with her. He had been very kind, Komako said, and it made her sad to think that she could not give her whole self to him. He was considerably older than she, and he but rarely came to see her.

"I sometimes think it would be easiest to break away from him if I were to be really bad. I honestly think so sometimes."

"That would never do."

"But I wouldn't be up to it. It's not in my nature. I'm fond of this body I live in. If I tried, I could cut my four years down to two, but I don't strain myself. I take care of myself. Think of all the money I could make if I really tried. But it's enough if the man I have my contract with hasn't lost money at the end of four years. I know about how much it takes each month for an installment on the loan, and interest, and taxes, and my own keep, and I don't strain myself to make more. If it's a party that doesn't seem worth the trouble, I slip off and go home, and they don't call me late at night even from the inn unless an old guest has asked especially for me. If I wanted to be extravagant, I could go on and on, but I work as the mood takes me. That's enough. I've already paid back more than half the money, and it's not a year yet. But even so I manage to spend thirty yen or so on myself every month."

It was enough if she made a hundred yen a month, she said. The month before, the least busy of the year, she had made sixty yen. She had had some ninety parties, more than any other geisha. She received a fixed amount for herself from each party, and the larger number of parties therefore meant relatively more for her and less for the man to whom she was indentured. But she moved busily from one to another as the spirit took her. There was not a single geisha at this hot spring who lost money and had to extend her contract.

Komako was up early the next morning. "I dreamed I was cleaning house for the woman who teaches flower-arranging, and I woke up."

She had moved the little dresser over to the window. In the mirror the mountains were red with autumn leaves, and the autumn sun was bright.

This time it was not Yoko he heard, Yoko calling through the door in that voice so clear he found it a little sad. Komako's clothes were brought rather by the little daughter of the man with whom she had her contract.

"What happened to the girl?" Shimamura asked.

Komako darted a quick glance at him. "She spends all her time at the cemetery. Over there at the foot of the ski course. See the buckwheat field —the white flowers? And the cemetery to the left of it?"

Shimamura went for a walk in the village when Komako had left.

Before a white wall, shaded by eaves, a little girl in "mountain trousers" and an orange-red flannel kimono, clearly brand-new, was bouncing a rubber ball. For Shimamura, there was autumn in the little scene.

The houses were built in the style of the old regime. No doubt they were there when provincial lords passed down this north-country road. The eaves and the verandas were deep, while the latticed, paper-covered windows on the second floor were long and low, no more than a foot or so high. There were reed blinds hanging from the eaves.

Slender autumn grasses grew along the top of an earthen wall. The pale-yellow plumes were at their most graceful, and below each plume narrow leaves spread out in a delicate fountain.

Yoko knelt on a straw mat beside the road, flailing at beans spread out before her in the sunlight.

The beans jumped from their dry pods like little drops of light.

Perhaps she could not see him because of the scarf around her head. She knelt, flailing away at the beans, her knees spread apart in their "mountain trousers," and she sang in that voice so clear it was almost sad, the voice that seemed to be echoing back from somewhere.

"The butterfly, the dragonfly, the cricket.
The pine cricket, bell cricket, horse cricket
Are singing in the hills."

How large the crow is, starting up from the cedar in the evening breeze—so says the poet. Again there were swarms of dragonflies by the cedar grove Shimamura could see from his window. As the evening approached, they seemed to swim about faster, more restlessly.

Shimamura had bought a new guide to these mountains while he was waiting for his train in Tokyo. Thumbing through it, he learned that near the top of one of the Border Range peaks a path threaded its way through beautiful lakes and marshes, and in this watery belt Alpine plants grew in the wildest profusion. In the summer red dragonflies flew calmly about, lighting on a hat or a hand, or the rim of a pair of spectacles, as different from the persecuted city dragonfly as a cloud from a mud puddle.

But the dragonflies here before him seemed to be driven by something. It was as though they wanted desperately to avoid being pulled in with the cedar grove as it darkened before the sunset.

The western sun fell on distant mountains, and in the evening light he could see how the red leaves were working their way down from the summits.

"People are delicate, aren't they?" Komako had said that morning. "Broken into a pulp, they say, skull and bones and all. And a bear could fall from a higher ledge and not be hurt in the least." There had been another accident up among the rocks, and she had pointed out the mountain on which it had happened.

If man had a tough, hairy hide like a bear, his world would be different indeed, Shimamura thought. It was through a thin, smooth skin that man loved. Looking out at the evening mountains, Shimamura felt a sentimental longing for the human skin.

"The butterfly, the dragonfly, the cricket." A geisha had been singing the song to a clumsy samisen accompaniment as he sat down to an early dinner.

The guidebook gave only the most essential information on routes, schedules, lodgings, costs, and left the rest to the imagination. Shimamura had come down from these mountains, as the new green was making its way through the last of the snow, to meet Komako for the first time; and now, in the autumn climbing season, he found himself drawn again to the mountains he had left his tracks in. Though he was an idler who might as well spend his time in the mountains as anywhere, he looked upon mountain climbing as almost a model of wasted effort. For that very reason it pulled at him with the attraction of the unreal.

When he was far away, he thought incessantly of Komako; but now that he was near her, this sighing for the human skin took on a dreamy quality like the spell of the mountains. Perhaps he felt a certain security, perhaps he was at the moment too intimate, too familiar with her body. She had stayed with him the night before. Sitting alone in the quiet, he could only wait for her. He was sure she would come without his calling. As he listened to the noisy chatter of a group of schoolgirls out on the hiking trip, however, he began to feel a little sleepy. He went to bed early.

Rain fell during the night, one of those quick showers that come in the autumn.

When he awoke the next morning, Komako was sitting primly beside the table, a book open before her. She wore an everyday kimono and cloak.

"Are you awake?" Her voice was soft as she turned to him.

"What are you doing here?"

"Are you awake?"

Shimamura glanced around the room, wonder-

ing if she had come in the night without his knowing it. He picked up the watch beside his pillow.
It was only six-thirty.

"You're early."

"But the maid has already brought charcoal."

A morninglike steam was rising from the tea-
kettle.

"It's time to get up." She sat beside his pillow, the picture of the proper housewife. Shimamura stretched and yawned. He took the hand on
her knee and caressed the small fingers, callused
from playing the samisen.

"But it's barely sunrise."

"Did you sleep well by yourself?"

"Very well."

"You didn't grow a mustache after all."

"You did tell me to grow a mustache, didn't
you?"

"It's all right. I knew you wouldn't. You always
shave yourself nice and blue."

"And you always look as if you'd just shaved
when you wash away that powder."

"Isn't your face a little fatter, though? You were
very funny asleep, all round and plump with your
white skin and no mustache."

"Sweet and gentle?"

"But unreliable."

"You were staring at me, then? I'm not sure I

like having people stare at me when I'm asleep."

Komako smiled and nodded. Then, like a glow
that breaks into a flame, the smile became a laugh.
There was strength in the fingers that took his.

"I hid in the closet. The maid didn't suspect a
thing."

"When? How long were you hidden?"

"Just now, of course. When the maid came to
bring charcoal." She laughed happily at the prank,
and suddenly she was red to the ears. As if to hide
her confusion, she began fanning herself with the
edge of his quilt. "Get up. Get up, please."

"It's cold." Shimamura pulled the quilt away
from her. "Are the inn people up yet?"

"I have no idea. I came in from the back."

"The back?"

"I fought my way up from the cedar grove."

"Is there a path in back?"

"No. But it's shorter."

Shimamura looked at her in surprise.

"No one knows I'm here. I heard someone in
the kitchen, but the front door must still be
locked."

"You seem to be an early riser."

"I couldn't sleep."

"Did you hear the rain?"

"It rained? That's why the underbrush was wet,
then. I'm going home. Go on back to sleep."

But Shimamura jumped vigorously out of bed, the woman's hand still in his. He went over to the window and looked down at the hill she said she had come up. Below the shrubbery, halfway down toward the cedar grove, dwarf bamboo was growing in a wild tangle. Directly below the window were rows of taro and sweet potatoes, onions and radishes. It was a most ordinary garden patch, and yet the varied colors of the leaves in the morning sun made him feel that he was seeing them for the first time.

The porter was throwing feed to the carp from the corridor that led to the bath.

"It's colder, and they aren't eating well," he said as Shimamura passed. Shimamura stood for a moment looking at the feed on the water, dried and crumbled silkworms.

Komako was waiting for him, clean and prim as before, when he came back from the bath.

"It would be good to work on my sewing in a quiet place like this," she said.

The room had evidently been cleaned, and the sun poured in on the deepest corners of the slightly worn matting.

"You sew, do you?"

"What an insulting question. I had to work harder than anyone else in the family. I see now, looking back, that the years when I was growing up were the worst ones of all." She spoke almost to herself, but her voice was tense as she continued: "The maid saw me. She gave me a strange look and asked when I had come. It was very embarrassing—but I couldn't go on hiding in the closet forever. I'm going home. I'm very busy. I couldn't sleep, and I thought I'd wash my hair. I have to wait for it to dry, and then go to the hairdresser's, and if I don't wash it early in the morning I'm never ready for an afternoon party. There's a party here too, but they only told me about it last night. I won't come. I've made other promises. And I won't be able to see you tonight— it's Saturday and I'll be very busy."

She showed no sign of leaving, however.

She decided not to wash her hair after all. She took Shimamura down to the back garden. Her damp sandals and stockings were hidden under the veranda where she had come in.

The dwarf bamboo she said she had fought her way through seemed impassible. Starting down along the garden path toward the sound of the water, they came out on the high river bank. There were children's voices in the chestnut trees. A number of burrs lay in the grass at their feet. Komako stamped them open and took out the fruit. The kernels were small.

Kaya plumes waved on the steep slope of the

mountain opposite, a dazzling silver in the morning sun. Dazzling, and yet rather like the fleeting
translucence that moved across the autumn sky.

"Shall we cross over? We can see your fiancé's
grave."

Komako brought herself to her full height and
glared at him. A handful of chestnuts came at his
face.

"You're making fun of me."

Shimamura had no time to dodge. The chestnuts lashed at his forehead.

"What possible reason could you have for going
to the cemetery?"

"But there's no need to lose your temper."

"I was completely in earnest. I'm not like people who can do exactly as they want and think of
no one else."

"And who can do that?" Shimamura muttered
weakly.

"Why do you have to call him my fiancé? Didn't
I tell you very carefully he wasn't? But you've forgotten, of course."

Shimamura had not forgotten. Indeed, the
memory gave the man Yukio a certain weight in
his thoughts.

Komako seemed to dislike talking about Yukio.
She was not his fiancée, perhaps, but she had become a geisha to help pay doctors' bills. There was

no doubt that she had been "completely in earnest."

Shimamura showed no anger even under the barrage of chestnuts. Komako looked curiously at him, and her resistance seemed to collapse. She took his arm. "You're a simple, honest person at heart, aren't you? Something must be making you sad."

"They're watching us from the trees."

"What of it? Tokyo people are complicated. They live in such noise and confusion that their feelings are broken to little bits."

"Everything is broken to little bits."

"Even life, before long. . . . Shall we go to the cemetery?"

"Well. . . ."

"See? You don't really want to go at all."

"But you made such an issue of it."

"Because I've never once gone to the cemetery. I really haven't gone once. I feel guilty sometimes, now that the teacher's buried there too. But I can't very well start going now. I'd only be pretending."

"You're more complicated than I am."

"Why? I'm never able to be completely open with living people, and I want at least to be honest with him now that he's dead."

They came out of the cedar grove, where the quiet seemed to fall in chilly drops. Following the railway along the foot of the ski grounds, they were soon at the cemetery. Some ten weathered old tombstones and a forlorn statue of Jizo, guardian of children, stood on a tiny island of high ground among the paddies. There were no flowers.

Quite without warning, Yoko's head and shoulders rose from the bushes behind the Jizo. Her face wore the usual solemn, masklike expression. She darted a burning glance at the two of them, and nodded a quick greeting to Shimamura. She said nothing.

"Aren't you early, though, Yoko? I thought of going to the hairdresser's. . . ." As Komako spoke, a black squall came upon them and threatened to sweep them from their feet.

A freight train roared past.

"Yoko, Yoko. . . ." A boy was waving his hat in the door of a black freight car.

"Saichiro, Saichiro," Yoko called back.

It was the voice that had called to the station master at the snowy signal stop, a voice so beautiful it was almost lonely, calling out as if to someone who could not hear, on a ship far away.

The train passed, and the buckwheat across the

tracks emerged fresh and clean as the blind was lifted. The field of white flowers on red stems was quietness itself.

The two of them had been so startled at seeing Yoko that they had not noticed the approach of the freight train; but the first shock was dispelled by the train.

They seemed still to hear Yoko's voice, and not the dying rumble of the freight train. It seemed to come back like an echo of distilled love.

"My brother," said Yoko, looking after the train. "I wonder if I should go to the station."

"But the train won't wait for you at the station," Komako laughed.

"I suppose not."

"I didn't come to see Yukio's grave."

Yoko nodded. She seemed to hesitate a moment, then knelt down before the grave.

Komako watched stiffly.

Shimamura looked away, toward the Jizo. It had three long faces, and, besides the hands clasped at its breast, a pair each to the left and the right.

"I'm going to wash my hair," Komako said to Yoko. She turned and started back along a ridge between the paddies.

It was the practice in the snow country to string wooden or bamboo poles on a number of levels from tree trunk to tree trunk, and to hang rice sheaves head down from them to dry. At the height of the harvest the frames presented a solid screen of rice. Farmers were hanging out rice along the path Shimamura and Komako took back to the village.

A farm girl threw up a sheaf of rice with a twist of her trousered hips, and a man high above her caught it expertly and in one deft sweep of his hand spread it to hang from the frame. The unconscious, practiced motions were repeated over and over.

Komako took one of the dangling sheaves in her hand and shook it gently up and down, as though she were feeling the weight of a jewel.

"See how it's headed. And how nice it is to the touch. Entirely different from last year's rice." She half-closed her eyes from the pleasure. A disorderly flock of sparrows flew low over her head.

An old notice was pasted to a wall beside the road: "Pay for field hands. Ninety sen a day, meals included. Women forty per cent less."

There were rice frames in front of Yoko's house too, beyond the slightly depressed field that separated the house from the road. One set of frames was strung up high in a row of persimmon trees, along the white wall between the garden and the house next door, while another, at right angles to it, followed the line between the field and the garden. With an opening for a doorway at one end, the frames suggested a makeshift little theater covered not with the usual straw mats but with unthreshed rice. The taro in the field still sent out powerful stems and leaves, but the dahlias and roses beyond were withered. The lotus pond with its red carp was hidden behind the screen of rice, as was the window of the silkworm room, where Komako had lived.

Bowing her head sharply, almost angrily, Yoko went in through the opening in the headed rice.

"Does she live alone?" Shimamura asked, looking after the bowed figure.

"I imagine not." Komako's answer was a little tart. "But what a nuisance. I'll not go to the hairdresser's after all. You say things you have no business saying, and we ruin her visit to the cemetery."

"You're only being difficult—is it really so terrible to run into her at the cemetery?"

"You have no idea how I feel. . . . If I have time later, I'll stop by to wash my hair. I may be late, but I'll stop by."

It was three in the morning.

Shimamura was awakened by a slamming as though someone were knocking the doors loose. Komako lay stretched out on top of him.

"I said I would come and I've come. Haven't I? I said I'd come and I've come, haven't I?" Her chest, even her abdomen, rose and fell violently.

"You're dead-drunk."

"Haven't I? I said I'd come and I've come, haven't I?"

"You have indeed."

"Couldn't see a thing on the way. Not a thing. My head aches."

"How did you manage to get up the hill?"

"I have no idea. Not the slightest." She lay heavily across his chest. He found it a little oppressive, especially when she turned over and arched her back; but, too suddenly awakened, he fell back as he tried to get up. It was an astonishingly hot object that his head came to rest on.

"You're on fire."

"Oh? Fire for a pillow. See that you don't burn yourself."

"I might very well." He closed his eyes and the warmth sank into his head, bringing an immediate sense of life. Reality came through the violent breathing, and with it a sort of nostalgic remorse. He felt as though he were waiting tranquilly for some undefined revenge.

"I said I'd come, and I've come." She spoke with the utmost concentration. "I've come, and now I'm going home. I'm going to wash my hair."

She got to her knees and took a drink of water in great swallows.

"I can't let you go home like this."

"I'm going home. I have some people waiting. Where did I leave my towel?"

Shimamura got up and turned on the light. "Don't!" She hid her face in her hands, then buried it, hands and all, in the quilt.

She had on a bold informal kimono with a narrow undress *obi*, and under it a nightgown. Her under-kimono had slipped down out of sight. She was flushed from drink even to the soles of her bare feet, and there was something very engaging about the way she tried to tuck them out of sight.

Evidently she had thrown down her towel and bath utensils when she came in. Soap and combs were scattered over the floor.

"Cut. I brought scissors."

"What do you want me to cut?"

"This." She pointed at the strings that held her Japanese coiffure in place. "I tried to do it myself, but my hands wouldn't work. I thought maybe I could ask you."

Shimamura separated the hair and cut at the strings, and as he cut she shook the long hair loose. She was somewhat calmer.

"What time is it?"

"Three o'clock."

"Not really! You'll be careful not to cut the hair, won't you?"

"I've never seen so many strings."

The false hair that filled out the coiffure was hot where it touched her head.

"Is it really three o'clock? I must have fallen asleep when I got home. I promised to come for a bath with some people, and they stopped by to call me. They'll be wondering what's happened."

"They're waiting for you?"

"In the public bath. Three of them. There were six parties, but I only got to four. Next week we'll be very busy with people coming to see the maple leaves. Thanks very much." She raised her head to comb her hair, now long and flowing, and she laughed uncertainly. "Funny, isn't it." Unsure what to do with herself, she reached to pick up the false hair. "I have to go. It's not right to keep them waiting. I'll not come again tonight."

"Can you see your way home?"

"Yes."

But she tripped over the skirt of her kimono on the way out.

At seven and again at three in the morning—twice in one short day she had chosen unconventional hours to come calling. There was something far from ordinary in all this, Shimamura told himself.

Guests would soon be coming for the autumn leaves. The door of the inn was being decorated with maple branches to welcome them.

The porter who was somewhat arrogantly directing operations was fond of calling himself a "migrant bird." He and his kind worked the mountain resorts from spring through to the autumn leaves, and moved down to the coast for the winter. He did not much care whether or not he came to the same inn each year. Proud of his experience in the prosperous coast resorts, he had no praise for the way the inn treated its guests. He reminded one of a not-too-sincere beggar as he rubbed his hands together and hovered about prospective guests at the station.

"Have you ever tasted one of these?" he asked Shimamura, picking up a pomegranatelike *akebi*. "I can bring some in from the mountains if you like." Shimamura, back from a walk, watched him tie the *akebi*, stem and all, to a maple branch.

The freshly cut branches were so long that they brushed against the eaves. The hallway glowed a bright, fresh scarlet. The leaves were extraordinarily large.

As Shimamura took the cool *akebi* in his hand,

he noticed that Yoko was sitting by the hearth in the office.

The innkeeper's wife was heating *saké* in a brass boiler. Yoko, seated opposite her, nodded quickly in answer to each remark. She was dressed informally, though she did not have on the everyday "mountain trousers." Her plain woolen kimono was freshly washed.

"That girl is working here?" Shimamura asked the porter nonchalantly.

"Yes, sir. Thanks to all of you, we've had to take on extra help."

"You, for instance."

"That's right. She's an unusual type, though, for a girl from these parts."

Yoko worked only in the kitchen, apparently. She was not yet serving at parties. As the inn filled, the voices of the maids in the kitchen became louder, but he did not remember having heard Yoko's clear voice among them. The maid who took care of his room said that Yoko liked to sing in the bath before she went to bed, but that, too, Shimamura had missed.

Now that he knew Yoko was in the house, he felt strangely reluctant to call Komako. He was conscious of an emptiness that made him see Komako's life as beautiful but wasted, even though he himself was the object of her love; and yet the woman's existence, her straining to live, came touching him like naked skin. He pitied her, and he pitied himself.

He was sure that Yoko's eyes, for all their innocence, could send a probing light to the heart of these matters, and he somehow felt drawn to her too.

Komako came often enough without being called.

When he went to see the maple leaves up the valley, he passed her house. Hearing the automobile and thinking it must be he, she ran out to look—and he did not even glance back, she complained. That was most unfeeling of him. She of course stopped by whenever she came to the inn, and she stopped by too on her way to the bath. When she was to go to a party, she came an hour or so early and waited in his room for the maid to call her. Often she would slip away from a party for a few minutes. After retouching her face in the mirror, she would stand up to leave. "Back to work. I'm all business. Business, business."

She was in the habit of forgetting something she had brought with her, a cloak, perhaps, or the cover to a samisen plectrum.

"Last night when I got home there was no hot water for tea. I hunted through the kitchen and

found the left-overs from breakfast. Co-o-old. . . .
They didn't call me this morning. When I woke
up it was already ten-thirty. I meant to come see
you at seven, but it was no good."

Such were the things she talked of. Or she told
him of the inn she had gone to first, and the next
and the next, and the parties she had been to at
each.

"I'll come again later." She had a glass of water
before she left. "Or maybe I won't. Thirty guests
and only three of us. I'll be much too busy."

But almost immediately she was back.

"It's hard work. Thirty of them and only three
of us. And the other two are the very oldest and
the very youngest in town, and that leaves all the
hard work for me. Stingy people. A travel club of
some sort, I suppose. With thirty guests you need
at least six geisha. I'll go have a drink and pick a
fight with them."

So it was every day. Komako must have wanted
to crawl away and hide at the thought of where
it was leading. But that indefinable air of loneliness only made her the more seductive.

"The floor always creaks when I come down the
hall. I walk very softly, but they hear me just the
same. 'Off to the Camellia Room again, Komako?'
they say as I go by the kitchen. I never thought
I'd have to worry so about my reputation."

"The town's really too small."

"Everyone has heard about us, of course."

"That will never do."

"You begin to have a bad name, and you're ruined in a little place like this." But she looked up and smiled. "It makes no difference. My kind can find work anywhere."

That straightforward manner, so replete with direct, immediate feeling, was quite foreign to Shimamura, the idler who had inherited his money.

"It will be the same, wherever I go. There's nothing to be upset about."

But he caught an echo of the woman underneath the surface nonchalance.

"And I can't complain. After all, only women are able really to love." She flushed a little and looked at the floor.

Her kimono stood out from her neck, and her back and shoulders were like a white fan spread under it. There was something sad about the full flesh under that white powder. It suggested a woolen cloth, and again it suggested the pelt of some animal.

"In the world as it is," he murmured, chilled at the sterility of the words even as he spoke.

But Komako only replied: "As it always has

been." She raised her head and added absent-mindedly: "You didn't know that?"

The red under-kimono clinging to her skin disappeared as she looked up.

Shimamura was translating Valéry and Alain, and French treatises on the dance from the golden age of the Russian ballet. He meant to bring them out in a small luxury edition at his own expense. The book would in all likelihood contribute nothing to the Japanese dancing world. One could nonetheless say, if pressed, that it would bring aid and comfort to Shimamura. He pampered himself with the somewhat whimsical pleasure of sneering at himself through his work, and it may well have been from such a pleasure that his sad little dream world sprang. Off on a trip, he saw no need to hurry himself.

He spent much of his time watching insects in their death agonies.

Each day, as the autumn grew colder, insects died on the floor of his room. Stiff-winged insects fell on their backs and were unable to get to their feet again. A bee walked a little and collapsed, walked a little and collapsed. It was a quiet death that came with the change of seasons. Looking closely, however, Shimamura could see that the legs and feelers were trembling in the struggle to live. For such a tiny death, the empty eight-mat room* seemed enormous.

As he picked up a dead insect to throw it out, he sometimes thought for an instant of the children he had left in Tokyo.

A moth on the screen was still for a very long time. It too was dead, and it fell to the earth like a dead leaf. Occasionally a moth fell from the wall. Taking it up in his hand, Shimamura would wonder how to account for such beauty.

The screens were removed, and the singing of the insects was more subdued and lonely day by day.

The russet deepened on the Border Range. In the evening sun the mountains lighted up sharply, like a rather chilly stone. The inn was filled with maple-viewing guests.

"I don't think I'll come again tonight. Some people from the village are having a party." Komako left, and presently he heard a drum in the large banquet-room, and strident women's voices. At the very height of the festivities he was startled by a clear voice almost at his elbow.

"May I come in?" It was Yoko. "Komako asked me to bring this."

She thrust her hand out like a postman. Then, remembering her manners, she knelt down awk-

* About four yards square.

wardly before him. Shimamura opened the knot-
ted bit of paper, and Yoko was gone. He had not
had time to speak to her.

"Having a fine, noisy time. And drinking."
That was the whole of the message, written in a
drunken hand on a paper napkin.

Not ten minutes later Komako staggered in.

"Did she bring something to you?"

"She did."

"Oh?" Komako cocked an eye at him in wonderfully high spirits. "I do feel good. I said I'd go
order more *saké*, and I ran away. The porter
caught me. But *saké* is wonderful. I don't care a
bit if the floor creaks. I don't care if they scold me.
As soon as I come here I start feeling drunk,
though. Damn. Well, back to work."

"You're rosy down to the tips of your fingers."

"Business is waiting. Business, business. Did she
say anything? Terribly jealous. Do you know how
jealous?"

"Who?"

"Someone will be murdered one of these days."

"She's working here?"

"She brings *saké*, and then stands there staring
in at us, with her eyes flashing. I suppose you like
her sort of eyes."

"She probably thinks you're a disgrace."

"That's why I gave her a note to bring to you.

I want water. Give me water. Who's a disgrace? Try seducing her too before you answer my question. Am I drunk?" She peered into the mirror, bracing both hands against the stand. A moment later, kicking aside the long skirts, she swept from the room.

The party was over. The inn was soon quiet, and Shimamura could hear a distant clatter of dishes. Komako must have been taken off by a guest to a second party, he concluded; but just then Yoko came in with another bit of paper.

"Decided not to go to Sampukan go from here to the Plum Room may stop by on way home good night."

Shimamura smiled wryly, a little uncomfortable before Yoko. "Thank you very much. You've come to help here?"

She darted a glance at him with those beautiful eyes, so bright that he felt impaled on them. His discomfort was growing.

The girl left a deep impression each time he saw her, and now she was sitting before him—a strange uneasiness swept over him. Her too-serious manner made her seem always at the very center of some remarkable occurrence.

"They're keeping you busy, I suppose."

"But there's very little I can do."

"It's strange how often I see you. The first time was when you were bringing that man home. You talked to the station master about your brother. Do you remember?"

"Yes."

"They say you sing in the bath before you go to bed."

"Really! They accuse me of having such bad manners?" The voice was astonishingly beautiful.

"I feel I know everything about you."

"Oh? And have you asked Komako, then?"

"She won't say a thing. She seems to dislike talking about you."

"I see." Yoko turned quickly away. "Komako is a fine person, but she's not been lucky. Be good to her." She spoke rapidly, and her voice trembled very slightly on the last words.

"But there's nothing I can do for her."

It seemed that the girl's whole body must soon be trembling. Shimamura looked away, fearful that a dangerous light would be breaking out on the too-earnest face.

He laughed. "I think I'd best go back to Tokyo soon."

"I'm going to Tokyo myself."

"When?"

"It doesn't matter."

"Shall I see you to Tokyo when I go back?"

"Please do." The seriousness was intense, and at the same time her tone suggested that the matter was after all trivial. Shimamura was startled.

"If it will be all right with your family."

"The brother who works on the railroad is all the family I have. I can decide for myself."

"Have you made arrangements in Tokyo?"

"No."

"Have you talked to Komako, then?"

"To Komako? I don't like Komako. I haven't talked to her."

She looked up at him with moist eyes—a sign perhaps that her defenses were breaking down—and he found in them an uncanny sort of beauty. But at that moment his affection for Komako welled up violently. To run off to Tokyo, as if eloping, with a nondescript woman would somehow be in the nature of an intense apology to Komako, and a penance for Shimamura himself.

"It doesn't frighten you to go off alone with a man?"

"Why should it?"

"It doesn't seem dangerous to go to Tokyo without at least deciding where you will stay and what you might want to do?"

"A woman by herself can always get by." There was a delicious lilt in her speech. Her eyes were fixed on his as she spoke again: "You won't hire me as a maid?"

"Really, now. Hire you as a maid?"

"But I don't want to be a maid."

"What were you in Tokyo before?"

"A nurse."

"You were in a hospital? Or in nursing school?"

"I just thought I'd like to be a nurse."

Shimamura smiled. This perhaps explained the earnestness with which she had taken care of the music teacher's son on the train.

"And you still want to be a nurse?"

"I won't be a nurse now."

"But you'll have to make up your mind. This indecisiveness will never do."

"Indecisiveness? It has nothing to do with indecisiveness." Her laugh threw back the accusation.

Her laugh, like her voice, was so high and clear that it was almost lonely. There was not a suggestion in it of the dull or the simple-minded; but it struck emptily at the shell of Shimamura's heart, and fell away in silence.

"What's funny?"

"But there has only been one man I could possibly nurse."

Again Shimamura was startled.

"I could never again."

"I see." His answer was quiet. He had been caught off guard. "They say you spend all your time at the cemetery."

"I do."

"And for the rest of your life you can never nurse anyone else, or visit anyone else's grave?"

"Never again."

"How can you leave the grave and go off to Tokyo, then?"

"I'm sorry. Do take me with you."

"Komako says you're frightfully jealous. Wasn't the man her fiancé?"

"Yukio? It's a lie. It's a lie."

"Why do you dislike Komako, then?"

"Komako." She spoke as if calling to someone in the same room, and she gazed hotly at Shimamura. "Be good to Komako."

"But I can do nothing for her."

There were tears in the corners of Yoko's eyes. She sniffled as she slapped at a small moth on the matting. "Komako says I'll go crazy." With that she slipped from the room.

Shimamura felt a chill come over him.

As he opened the window to throw out the moth, he caught a glimpse of the drunken Komako playing parlor games with a guest. She leaned forward half from her seat, as though to push her advantage home by force. The sky had clouded over. Shimamura went down for a bath.

In the women's bath next door, Yoko was bathing the innkeeper's little daughter.

Her voice was gentle as she undressed the child and bathed it—soothing and agreeable, like the voice of a young mother.

Presently she was singing in that same voice:

> "See, *out in back,*
> *Three pears, three cedars,*
> *Six trees in all.*
> *Crows' nests below,*
> *Sparrows' nests above.*
> *And what is it they're singing?*
> 'Hakamairi itchō, itchō, itchō ya.' " *

It was a song little girls sang as they bounced rubber balls. The quick, lively manner in which Yoko rolled off the nonsense-words made Shimamura wonder if he might not have seen the earlier Yoko in a dream.

She chattered on as she dressed the child and led it from the bath, and even when she was gone her voice seemed to echo on like a flute. On

---

* In imitation of the birds. Literally: "To the cemetery, a hundred yards, a hundred yards, a hundred yards again."

the worn floor of the hallway, polished to a dark glow, a geisha had left behind a samisen box, the very embodiment of quiet in the late autumn night. As Shimamura was looking for the owner's name, Komako came out from the direction of the clattering dishes.

"What are you looking at?"

"Is she staying the night?"

"Who? Oh, her. Don't be foolish. You think we carry these with us wherever we go, do you? Sometimes we leave them at an inn for days on end." She laughed, but almost immediately she was breathing painfully and her eyes were screwed tightly shut. Dropping her long skirts, she fell against Shimamura. "Take me home, please."

"You don't have to go, do you?"

"It's no good. I have to go. The rest went on to other parties and left me behind. No one will say anything if I don't stay too long—I had business here. But if they stop by my house on their way to the bath and find me away, they'll start talking."

Drunk though she was, she walked briskly down the steep hill.

"You made that girl weep."

"She does seem a trifle crazy."

"And do you enjoy making such remarks?"

"But didn't you say it yourself? She remembered how you said she would go crazy, and it was then that she broke down—mostly out of resentment, I suspect."

"Oh? It's all right, then."

"And not ten minutes later she was in the bath, singing in fine voice."

"She's always liked to sing in the bath."

"She said very seriously that I must be good to you."

"Isn't she foolish, though? But you didn't have to tell me."

"Tell you? Why is it that you always seem so touchy when that girl is mentioned?"

"Would you like to have her?"

"See? What call is there for a remark like that?"

"I'm not joking. Whenever I look at her, I feel as though I have a heavy load and can't get rid of it. Somehow I always feel that way. If you're really fond of her, take a good look at her. You'll see what I mean." She laid her hand on his shoulder and leaned toward him. Then, abruptly, she shook her head. "No, that's not what I want. If she were to fall into the hands of someone like you, she might not go crazy after all. Why don't you take my load for me?"

"You're going a little too far."

"You think I'm drunk and talking nonsense? I'm not. I would know she was being well taken care of, and I could go pleasantly to seed here in the mountains. It would be a fine, quiet feeling."

"That's enough."

"Just leave me alone." In her flight, she ran into the closed door of the house she lived in.

"They've decided you're not coming home."

"But I can open it." The door sounded old and dry as she lifted it from the groove and pushed it back.

"Come on in."

"But think of the hour."

"Everyone will be asleep."

Shimamura hesitated.

"I'll see you back to the inn, then."

"I can go by myself."

"But you haven't seen my room."

They stepped through the kitchen door, and the sleeping figures of the family lay sprawled before them. The thin mattresses on the floor were covered with cheap striped cloth, now faded, of the sort often used for "mountain trousers." The mother and father and five or six children, the oldest a girl perhaps sixteen, lay under a scorched lampshade. Heads faced in every direction. There was drab poverty in the scene, and yet under it there lay an urgent, powerful vitality.

As if thrown back by the warm breath of all the sleepers, Shimamura started toward the door.

Komako noisily closed it in his face, however, and went in through the kitchen. She made no attempt to soften her footsteps. Shimamura followed stealthily past the children's pillows, a strange thrill rising in his chest.

"Wait here. I'll turn on the light upstairs."

"It's all right." Shimamura climbed the stairs in the dark. As he looked back, he saw the candy shop beyond the homely sleeping faces.

The matting was worn in the four rustic rooms on the second floor.

"It's a little large, I have to admit, for just one person." The partitions between the rooms had been taken down, and Komako's bedding lay small and solitary inside the sliding doors, their paper panels yellowed with age, that separated the rooms from the skirting corridor. Old furniture and tools, evidently the property of the family she lived with, were piled in the far room. Party kimonos hung from pegs along the wall. The whole suggested a fox's or badger's lair to Shimamura.

Komako sat down solidly in the slightly raised alcove and offered him the only cushion.

"Bright red." She peered into the mirror. "Am I really so drunk?" She fumbled through the top drawer of the dresser. "Here. My diary."

"As long as this, is it?"

She took up a small figured-paper box filled to the top with assorted cigarettes.

"I push them up my sleeve or inside my *obi* when a guest gives them to me, and some of them are a little smashed. They're clean, though. I make up for wrinkles by having every variety to offer." She stirred up the contents to demonstrate that he could have his choice.

"But I don't have a match. I don't need matches now that I've stopped smoking."

"It's all right. How is the sewing?"

"I try to work at it, but the guests for the maple leaves keep me busy." She turned to put away the sewing that lay in front of the dresser.

The fine-grained chest of drawers and the expensive vermilion-lacquered sewing-box, relics perhaps of her years in Tokyo, were as they had been in the attic that so resembled an old paper box; but they seemed sadly out of place in these dilapidated second-floor rooms.

A thin string ran from Komako's pillow to the ceiling.

"I turn the light out with this when I'm reading." She tugged at the string. Gentle and subdued, the proper housewife again, she was not quite able even so to hide her discomposure.

"Lonely as the fox's lady out at night, aren't you."

"I really am."

"And do you mean to live here four years?"

"But it's going on a year already. It won't be long."

Shimamura was nervous. He thought he could hear the breathing of the family below, and he had run out of things to talk about. He stood up to leave.

Komako slid the door half shut behind him. She glanced up at the sky. "It's beginning to look like snow. The end of the maple leaves." She recited a line of poetry* as she stepped outside: "Here in our mountains, the snow falls even on the maple leaves."

"Well, good night."

"Wait. I'll see you back to the hotel. As far as the door, no farther."

But she followed him inside.

"Go on to bed." She slipped away, and a few minutes later she was back with two glasses filled to the brim with *saké*.

"Drink," she ordered as she stepped into the room. "We're going to have a drink."

"But aren't they asleep? Where did you find it?"

"I know where they keep it." She had quite obviously had herself a drink as she poured from

* The line is from a Kabuki play.

the vat. The earlier drunkenness had come back. With narrowed eyes, she watched the *saké* spill over on her hand. "It's no fun, though, swallowing the stuff down in the dark."

Shimamura drank meekly from the cup that was thrust at him.

It was not usual for him to get drunk on so little; but perhaps he was chilled from the walk. He began to feel sick. His head was whirling, and he could almost see himself going pale. He closed his eyes and fell back on the quilt. Komako put her arms around him in alarm. A childlike feeling of security came to him from the warmth of her body.

She seemed ill at ease, like a young woman, still childless, who takes a baby up in her arms. She raised her head and looked down, as at the sleeping child.

"You're a good girl."

"Why? Why am I good? What's good about me?"

"You're a good girl."

"Don't tease me. It's wrong of you." She looked aside, and she spoke in broken phrases, like little blows, as she rocked him back and forth.

She laughed softly to herself.

"I'm not good at all. It's not easy having you here. You'd best go home. Each time I come to see you I want to put on a new kimono, and now I have none left. This one is borrowed. So you see I'm not really good at all."

Shimamura did not answer.

"And what do you find good in me?" Her voice was a little husky. "The first day I met you I thought I had never seen anyone I disliked more. People just don't say the sort of things you said. I hated you."

Shimamura nodded.

"Oh? You understand then why I've not mentioned it before? When a woman has to say these things, she has gone as far as she can, you know."

"But it's all right."

"Is it?" They were silent for some moments. Komako seemed to be looking back on herself, and the awareness of a woman's being alive came to Shimamura in her warmth.

"You're a good woman."

"How am I good?"

"A good woman."

"What an odd person." Her face was hidden from him, as though she were rubbing her jaw against an itching shoulder. Then suddenly, Shimamura had no idea why, she raised herself angrily to an elbow.

"A good woman—what do you mean by that? What do you mean?"

He only stared at her.

"Admit it. That's why you came to see me. You were laughing at me. You were laughing at me after all."

She glared at him, scarlet with anger. Her shoulders were shaking. But the flush receded as quickly as it had come, and tears were falling over her blanched face.

"I hate you. How I hate you." She rolled out of bed and sat with her back to him.

Shimamura felt a stabbing in his chest as he saw what the mistake had been. He lay silent, his eyes closed.

"It makes me very sad," she murmured to herself. Her head was on her knees, and her body was bent into a tight ball.

When she had wept herself out, she sat jabbing at the floor mat with a silver hair-ornament. Presently she slipped from the room.

Shimamura could not bring himself to follow her. She had reason to feel hurt.

But soon she was back, her bare feet quiet in the corridor. "Are you going for a bath?" she called from outside the door. It was a high, thin little voice.

"If you want."

"I'm sorry. I've reconsidered."

She showed no sign of coming in. Shimamura

picked up his towel and stepped into the hall. She walked ahead of him with her eyes on the floor, like a criminal being led away. As the bath warmed her, however, she became strangely gay and winsome, and sleep was out of the question.

The next morning Shimamura awoke to a voice reciting a Nō play.

He lay for a time listening. Kamoko turned and smiled from the mirror.

"The guests in the Plum Room. I was called there after my first party. Remember?"

"A Nō club out on a trip?"

"Yes."

"It snowed?"

"Yes." She got up and threw open the sliding door in front of the window. "No more maple leaves."

From the gray sky, framed by the window, the snow floated toward them in great flakes, like white peonies. There was something quietly un-real about it. Shimamura stared with the vacant-ness that comes from lack of sleep.

The Nō reciters had taken out a drum.

He remembered the snowy morning toward the end of the year before, and glanced at the mirror. The cold peonies floated up yet larger, cutting a white outline around Komako. Her kimono was open at the neck, and she was wiping at her throat with a towel.

Her skin was as clean as if it had just been laundered. He had not dreamed that she was a woman who would find it necessary to take offense at such a trivial remark, and that very fact lent her an irresistible sadness.

The mountains, more distant each day as the russet of the autumn leaves had darkened, came brightly back to life with the snow.

The cedars, under a thin coating of snow, rose sheer from the white ground to the sky, each cut off sharply from the rest.

The thread was spun in the snow, and the cloth woven in the snow, washed in the snow, and bleached in the snow. Everything, from the first spinning of the thread to the last finishing touches, was done in the snow. "There is Chijimi linen because there is snow," someone wrote long ago. "Snow is the mother of Chijimi."

The Chijimi grass-linen of this snow country was the handwork of the mountain maiden through the long, snowbound winters. Shimamura searched for the cloth in old-clothes shops to use for summer kimonos. Through acquaintances in the dance world, he had found a shop that specialized in old Nō robes, and he had a standing order that when a good piece of Chijimi came in he was to see it.

In the old days, it is said, the early Chijimi fair was held in the spring, when the snow had melted and the snow blinds were taken down from the houses. People came from far and near to buy Chijimi, even wholesalers from the great commercial cities, Edo, Nagoya, and Osaka; and the inns at which they stayed were fixed by tradition. Since the labors of half a year were on display, youths and maidens gathered from all the mountain villages. Sellers' booths and buyers' booths were lined up side by side, and the market took on the air of a festival. With prizes awarded for the best pieces of weaving, it came also to be sort of competition for husbands. The girls learned to weave as children, and they turned out their best work between the ages of perhaps fourteen and twenty-four. As they grew older they lost the touch that gave tone to the finest Chijimi. In their desire to be numbered among the few outstanding weavers, they put their whole labor and love into this product of the long snowbound months—the months of seclusion and boredom, between October, under the old lunar calender, when the spinning began, and mid-February of the following year, when the last bleaching was finished.

There may have been among Shimamura's kimonos one or more woven by these mountain maidens toward the middle of the last century.

He still sent his kimonos back for "snow-bleaching." It was a great deal of trouble to return old kimonos—that had touched the skin of he could not know whom—for rebleaching each year to the country that had produced them; but when he considered the labors of those mountain maidens, he wanted the bleaching to be done properly in the country where the maidens had lived. The thought of the white linen, spread out on the deep snow, the cloth and the snow glowing scarlet in the rising sun, was enough to make him feel that the dirt of the summer had been washed away, even that he himself had been bleached clean. It must be added, however, that a Tokyo shop took care of the details for him, and he had no way of knowing that the bleaching had really been done in the old manner.

From ancient times there were houses that specialized in bleaching. The weavers for the most part did not do their own. White Chijimi was spread out on the snow after it was woven, colored Chijimi bleached on frames while still in thread. The bleaching season came in January and February under the lunar calendar, and snow-covered fields and gardens were the bleaching grounds.

The cloth or thread was soaked overnight in ash water. The next morning it was washed over and over again, wrung, and put out to bleach. The process was repeated day after day, and the sight when, as the bleaching came to an end, the rays of the rising sun turned the white Chijimi blood-red was quite beyond description, Shimamura had read in an old book. It was something to be shown to natives of warmer provinces. And the end of the bleaching was a sign that spring was coming to the snow country.

The land of the Chijimi was very near this hot spring, just down the river, where the valley began to widen out. Indeed it must almost have been visible from Shimamura's window. All of the Chijimi market towns now had railway stations, and the region was still a well-known weaving center.

Since Shimamura had never come to the snow country in midsummer, when he wore Chijimi, or in the snowy season, when it was woven, he had never had occasion to talk of it to Komako; and she hardly seemed the person to ask about the fate of an old folk art.

When he heard the song Yoko sang in the bath, it had come to him that, had she been born long ago, she might have sung thus as she worked over her spools and looms, so exactly suited to the fancy was her voice.

The thread of the grass-linen, finer than animal hair, is difficult to work except in the humidity of the snow, it is said, and the dark, cold season is therefore ideal for weaving. The ancients used to add that the way this product of the cold has of feeling cool to the skin in the hottest weather is a play of the principles of light and darkness. This Komako too, who had so fastened herself to him, seemed at center cool, and the remarkable, con-centrated warmth was for that fact all the more touching.

But this love would leave behind it nothing so definite as a piece of Chijimi. Though cloth to be worn is among the most short-lived of craftworks, a good piece of Chijimi, if it has been taken care of, can be worn quite unfaded a half-century and more after weaving. As Shimamura thought ab-sently how human intimacies have not even so long a life, the image of Komako as the mother of another man's children suddenly floated into his mind. He looked around, startled. Possibly he was tired.

He had stayed so long that one might wonder whether he had forgotten his wife and children. He stayed not because he could not leave Komako nor because he did not want to. He had simply fallen into the habit of waiting for those frequent visits. And the more continuous the assault became, the more he began to wonder what was lacking in him, what kept him from living as completely. He stood gazing at his own coldness, so to speak. He could not understand how she had so lost herself. All of Komako came to him, but it seemed that nothing went out from him to her. He heard in his chest, like snow piling up, the sound of Komako, an echo beating against empty walls. And he knew that he could not go on pampering himself forever.

He leaned against the brazier, provided against the coming of the snowy season, and thought how unlikely it was that he would come again once he had left. The innkeeper had lent him an old Kyoto teakettle, skillfully inlaid in silver with flowers and birds, and from it came the sound of wind in the pines. He could make out two pine breezes, as a matter of fact, a near one and a far one. Just beyond the far breeze he heard faintly the tinkling of a bell. He put his ear to the kettle and listened. Far away, where the bell tinkled on, he suddenly saw Komako's feet, tripping in time with the bell. He drew back. The time had come to leave.

He thought of going to see the Chijimi country. That excursion might set him on his way toward breaking away from this hot spring.

He did not know at which of the towns down-stream he should get off the train. Not interested in modern weaving centers, he chose a station that looked suitably lonesome and backward. After walking for a time he came out on what seemed to be the main street of an old post town.

The eaves pushing out far beyond the houses were supported by pillars along both sides of the street, and in their shade were passages for communication when the snow was deep, rather like the open lean-to the old Edo shopkeeper used for displaying his wares. With deep eaves on one side of each house, the passages stretched on down the street.

Since the houses were joined in a solid block, the snow from the roofs could only be thrown down into the street. One might more accurately say that at its deepest the snow was thrown not down but up, to a high bank of snow in the middle of the street. Tunnels were cut through for passage from one side to the other.

The houses in Komako's hot-spring village, for all of its being a part of this same snow country, were separated by open spaces, and this was therefore the first time Shimamura had seen the snow passages. He tried walking in one of them. The shade under the old eaves was dark, and the leaning pillars were beginning to rot at their bases. He walked along looking into the houses as into the gloom where generation after generation of his ancestors had endured the long snows.

He saw that the weaver maidens, giving themselves up to their work here under the snow, had lived lives far from as bright and fresh as the Chijimi they made. With an allusion to a Chinese poem, Shimamura's old book had pointed out that in harsh economic terms the making of Chijimi was quite impractical, so great was the expenditure of effort that went into even one piece. It followed that none of the Chijimi houses had been able to hire weavers from outside.

The nameless workers, so diligent while they lived, had presently died, and only the Chijimi remained, the plaything of men like Shimamura, cool and fresh against the skin in the summer. This rather unremarkable thought struck him as most remarkable. The labor into which a heart has poured its whole love—where will it have its say, to excite and inspire, and when?

Like the old post road that was its ancestor, the main street ran without a curve through the straggling village, and no doubt on through Komako's hot spring. The roofs, with rows of stones to weigh down their shingles, were very much like the ones he already knew.

The pillars supporting the deep eaves cast dim

shadows across the ground. With his hardly having noticed, afternoon had drawn on toward evening.

There was nothing more to see. He took a train to another village, very much like the first. Again he walked about for a time. Feeling a little chilly, he stopped for a bowl of noodles.

The noodle shop stood beside a river, probably the river that flowed past the hot spring. Shaven-headed Buddhist nuns were crossing a bridge in twos and threes to the far side. All wore rough straw sandals, and some had dome-shaped straw hats tied to their backs. Evidently on their way from a service, they looked like crows hurrying home to their nests.

"Quite a procession of them," Shimamura said to the woman who kept the shop.

"There's a nunnery up in the hills. I suppose they're getting everything done now. It will be next to impossible for them to go out once the heavy snows begin."

The mountain beyond the bridge, growing dark in the twilight, was already covered with snow.

In this snow country, cold, cloudy days succeed one another as the leaves fall and the winds grow chilly. Snow is in the air. The high mountains near and far become white in what the people of the country call "the round of the peaks." Along the coast the sea roars, and inland the mountains roar —"the roaring at the center," like a distant clap of thunder. The round of the peaks and the roaring at the center announce that the snows are not far away. This too Shimamura had read in his old book.

The first snow had fallen the morning he lay in bed listening to the Nō recital. Had the roaring already been heard, then, in the sea and the mountains? Perhaps his senses were sharper, off on a trip with only the company of the woman Komako: even now he seemed to catch an echo of a distant roaring.

"They'll be snowbound too, will they? How many are there?"

"A great many."

"What do they do with themselves, do you suppose, shut up together through the snows? Maybe we could set them to making Chijimi."

The woman smiled vaguely at the inquisitive stranger.

Shimamura went back to the station and waited two hours for a train. The wintry sun set, and the air was so clear that it seemed to burnish the stars. Shimamura's feet were cold.

He arrived back at the hot spring not knowing

what he had gone out looking for. The taxi crossed the tracks into the village as usual. A brightly lighted house stood before them as they skirted the cedar grove. Shimamura felt warm and safe again. It was the restaurant Kikumura, and three or four geisha were talking in the doorway.

Komako will be among them—but almost before he had time to frame the thought he saw only Komako.

The driver put on the brakes. Apparently he had heard rumors about the two.

Shimamura turned away from her to look out the rear window. In the light of the stars, the tracks were clear against the snow, surprisingly far into the distance.

Komako closed her eyes and jumped at the taxi. It moved slowly up the hill without stopping. She stood on the running-board, hunched over the door handle.

She had leaped at the car as if to devour it, but for Shimamura something warm had suddenly come near. The impulsive act struck him as neither rash nor unnatural. Komako raised one arm, half-embracing the closed window. Her kimono sleeve fell back from her wrist, and the warm red of the under-kimono, spilling through the thick glass, sank its way into the half-frozen Shimamura.

She pressed her forehead to the window.

"Where have you been? Tell me where you've been," she called in a high voice.

"Don't be a fool. You'll get hurt," he shouted back, but they both knew it was only a gentle game.

She opened the door and fell inside the taxi. It had already stopped, however. They were at the foot of the path up the mountain.

"Where have you been?"

"Well. . . ."

"Where?"

"Nowhere in particular."

He noticed with surprise that she had the geisha's way of arranging her skirts.

The driver waited silently. It was a bit odd, Shimamura had to admit, for them to be sitting in a taxi that had gone as far as it could.

"Let's get out." Komako put her hand on his. "Cold. See how cold. Why didn't you take me with you?"

"You think I should have?"

"What a strange person." She laughed happily as she hurried up the stone steps. "I saw you leave. About two . . . a little before three?"

"That's right."

"I ran out when I heard the car. I ran out in front. And you didn't look around."

"Look around?"

"You didn't. Why didn't you look around?"

Shimamura was a little surprised at this insistence.

"You didn't know I was seeing you off, did you?"

"I didn't."

"See?" Laughing happily to herself, she came very near him. "Why didn't you take me along? You leave me behind and you come back cold—I don't like it at all."

Suddenly a fire-alarm was ringing, with the special fury that told of an emergency.

They looked back.

"Fire, fire!"

"A fire!"

A column of sparks was rising in the village below.

Komako cried out two or three times, and clutched at Shimamura's hand.

A tongue of flames shot up intermittently in the spiral of smoke, dipping down to lick at the roofs about it.

"Where is it? Fairly near the music teacher's?"

"No."

"Where, then?"

"Farther up toward the station."

The tongue of flame sprang high over the roofs.

"It's the cocoon-warehouse. The warehouse. Look, look! The cocoon-warehouse is on fire." She pressed her face to his shoulder. "The warehouse, the warehouse!"

The fire blazed higher. From the mountain, however, it was as quiet under the starry sky as a little make-believe fire. Still the terror of it came across to them. They could almost hear the roar of the flames. Shimamura put his arm around Komako's shoulders.

"What is there to be afraid of?"

"No, no, no!" Komako shook her head and burst into tears. Her face seemed smaller than usual in Shimamura's hand. The hard forehead was trembling.

She had burst out weeping at the sight of the fire, and Shimamura held her to him without thinking to wonder what had so upset her.

She stopped weeping as quickly as she had begun, and pulled away from him.

"There's a movie in the warehouse. Tonight. The place will be full of people. . . . People will be hurt. People will burn to death."

They hurried up toward the inn. There was shouting above them. Guests stood on the second- and third-floor verandas, flooded with light from the open doors. At the edge of the garden, withering chrysanthemums were silhouetted against the light from the inn—or the starlight. For an instant he almost thought it was the light from the fire.

Several figures stood beyond the chrysanthemums. The porter and two or three others came bounding down the steps.

"Is it the cocoon-warehouse?" Komako called after them.

"That's right."

"Is anyone hurt? Has anyone been hurt?"

"They're getting everyone out. The film caught fire, and in no time the whole place was on fire. Heard it over the telephone. Look!" The porter raised one arm as he ran off. "Throwing children over one after another from the balcony, they say."

"What shall we do?" Komako started off down the stairs after the porter. Several others overtook her, and she too broke into a run. Shimamura followed.

At the foot of the stairs, their uneasiness increased. Only the very tip of the flames showed over the roofs, and the fire-alarm was nearer and more urgent.

"Careful. It's frozen, and you might slip." She stopped as she turned to look back at him. "But it's all right. You don't need to go any farther. I ought to go on myself to see if anyone has been hurt."

There was indeed no reason for him to go on. His excitement fell away. He looked down at his feet and saw that they had come to the crossing.

"The Milky Way. Beautiful, isn't it," Komako

murmured. She looked up at the sky as she ran off ahead of him.

The Milky Way. Shimamura too looked up, and he felt himself floating into the Milky Way. Its radiance was so near that it seemed to take him up into it. Was this the bright vastness the poet Bashō saw when he wrote of the Milky Way arched over a stormy sea? The Milky Way came down just over there, to wrap the night earth in its naked embrace. There was a terrible voluptuousness about it. Shimamura fancied that his own small shadow was being cast up against it from the earth. Each individual star stood apart from the rest, and even the particles of silver dust in the luminous clouds could be picked out, so clear was the night. The limitless depth of the Milky Way pulled his gaze up into it.

"Wait, wait," Shimamura called.

"Come on." Komako ran toward the dark mountain on which the Milky Way was falling.

She seemed to have her long skirts in her hands, and as her arms waved the skirts rose and fell a little. He could feel the red over the starlit snow.

He ran after her as fast as he could.

She slowed down and took his hand, and the long skirts fell to the ground. "You're going too?"

"Yes."

"Always looking for excitement." She clutched

at her skirts, now trailing over the snow. "But people will laugh. Please go back."

"Just a little farther."

"But it's wrong. People won't like it if I take you to a fire."

He nodded and stopped. Her hand still rested lightly on his sleeve, however, as she walked on.

"Wait for me somewhere. I'll be right back. Where will you wait?"

"Wherever you say."

"Let's see. A little farther." She peered into his face, and abruptly shook her head. "No. I don't want you to."

She threw herself against him. He reeled back a step or two. A row of onions was growing in the thin snow beside the road.

"I hated it." That sudden torrent of words came at him again. "You said I was a good woman, didn't you? You're going away. Why did you have to say that to me?"

He could see her stabbing at the mat with that silver hair-ornament.

"I cried about it. I cried again after I got home. I'm afraid to leave you. But please go away. I won't forget that you made me cry."

A feeling of nagging, hopeless impotence came over Shimamura at the thought that a simple misunderstanding had worked its way so deep into the woman's being. But just then they heard shouts from the direction of the fire, and a new burst of flame sent up its column of sparks.

"Look. See how it's flaming up again."

They ran on, released.

Komako ran well. Her sandals skimmed the frozen snow, and her arms, close to her sides, seemed hardly to move. She was as one whose whole strength is concentrated in the breast—a strangely small figure, Shimamura thought. Too plump for running himself, he was exhausted the more quickly from watching her. But Komako too was soon out of breath. She fell against him.

"My eyes are watering," she said. "That's how cold it is."

Shimamura's eyes too were moist. His cheeks were flushed, and only his eyes were cold. He blinked, and the Milky Way came to fill them. He tried to keep the tears from spilling over.

"Is the Milky Way like this every night?"

"The Milky Way? Beautiful, isn't it? But it's not like this every night. It's not usually so clear."

The Milky Way flowed over them in the direction they were running, and seemed to bathe Komako's head in its light.

The shape of her slightly aquiline nose was not clear, and the color was gone from her small lips. Was it so dim, then, the light that cut across the

sky and overflowed it? Shimamura found that
hard to believe. The light was dimmer even than
on the night of the new moon, and yet the Milky
Way was brighter than the brightest full moon. In
the faint light that left no shadows on the earth,
Komako's face floated up like an old mask. It was
strange that even in the mask there should be the
scent of the woman.

He looked up, and again the Milky Way came
down to wrap itself around the earth.

And the Milky Way, like a great aurora, flowed
through his body to stand at the edges of the
earth. There was a quiet, chilly loneliness in it,
and a sort of voluptuous astonishment.

"If you leave, I'll lead an honest life," Komako
said, walking on again. She put her hand to her
disordered hair. When she had gone five or six
steps she turned to look back at him. "What's the
matter? You don't have to stand there, do you?"

But Shimamura stood looking at her.

"Oh? You'll wait, then? And afterwards you'll
take me to your room with you."

She raised her left hand a little and ran off. Her
retreating figure was drawn up into the mountain.
The Milky Way spread its skirts to be broken by
the waves of the mountain, and, fanning out again
in all its brilliant vastness higher in the sky, it left
the mountain in a deeper darkness.

Komako turned into the main street and disappeared. Shimamura started after her.

Several men were pulling a fire-pump down the street to a rhythmical chant. Floods of people poured after them. Shimamura joined the crowd from the side road he and Komako had taken.

Another pump came down the street. He let it pass, and fell in behind it.

It was an old wooden hand-pump, ridiculously small, with swarms of men at the long rope pulling it and other swarms to man it.

Komako too had stopped to let it pass. She spotted Shimamura and ran along beside him. All down the road people who had stood aside fell in again as if sucked up by the pump. The two of them were now no more than part of a mob running to a fire.

"So you came. Always looking for excitement."

"That's right. It's a sad little pump, though, isn't it. The better part of a hundred years old."

"At least. Careful you don't fall."

"It is slippery."

"Come sometime when we have a real blizzard, and the snow drives along the ground all night long. But you won't, of course. Rabbits and pheasants come running inside the house to get out of the storm." Komako's voice was bright and eager. She seemed to take her beat from the chanting

voices and the tramping feet around her. Shimamura too was buoyed up by the crowd.

They could hear the sound of the flames now,
and tongues of flame leaped up before them. Komako clutched at Shimamura's arm. The low, dark
houses along the street seemed to be breathing as
they floated up in the light of the fire and faded
away again. Water from the pumps flowed along
the street. They came against a wall of people.
Mixed in with the smoke was a smell like boiling
cocoons.

The same standard remarks were taken up in
loud voices through the crowd: the fire had
started at the projector; children had been thrown
one after another from the balcony; no one was
hurt; it was lucky there had been no rice or cocoons in the warehouse. And yet a sort of quiet
unified the whole fiery scene, as though everyone
were voiceless before the flames, as though the
heart, the point of reference, had been torn away
from each individual. Everyone seemed to be listening to the sound of the fire and the pumps.

Now and then a villager came running up late,
and called out the name of a relative. There would
be an answer, and the two would call happily back
and forth. Only those voices seemed alive and
present. The fire-alarm no longer sounded.

Afraid people would be watching, Shimamura

slipped away from Komako and stood behind a group of children. The children moved back from the heat. The snow at their feet was melting, while farther on it had already turned to slush from the fire and water, a muddy confusion of footprints.

They were standing in the field beside the cocoon-warehouse. Most of the crowd on the main street had poured into that same open space.

The fire had apparently started near the entrance, and the walls and roof of half the building had burned away. The pillars and beams were still smoldering. It was a wide barn of a building, only shingles and boarded walls and floors, and the inside was fairly free of smoke. Though the roof, soaked from the pumps, did not seem to be burning, the fire continued to spread. A tongue would shoot up from a quite unexpected spot, the three pumps would turn hastily towards it, and a shower of sparks would fly up in a cloud of black smoke.

The sparks spread off into the Milky Way, and Shimamura was pulled up with them. As the smoke drifted away, the Milky Way seemed to dip and flow in the opposite direction. Occasionally a pump missed the roof, and the end of its line of water wavered and turned to a faint white mist, as though lighted by the Milky Way.

Komako had come up to him, he did not know

when. She took his hand. He looked around at her, but said nothing. She gazed at the fire, the pulse of the fire beating on her intent, slightly flushed face. Shimamura felt a violent rising in his chest. Komako's hair was coming undone, and her throat was bare and arched. His fingers trembled from the urge to touch it. His hand was warm, but Komako's was still warmer. He did not know why he should feel that a separation was forcing itself upon them.

Flames shot up again from the pillars and beams at the entrance. A line of water was turned on them. Hissing clouds of steam arose as the framework began to give way.

The crowd gasped as one person. A woman's body had fallen through the flames.

The cocoon-warehouse had a balcony that was little more than a perfunctory recognition of its duties as an auditorium. Since it fell from the balcony, low for a second floor, the body could have taken but a fraction of a second to reach the ground; but the eye had somehow been able to trace its passage in detail. Perhaps the strange, puppetlike deadness of the fall was what made that fraction of a second seem so long. One knew immediately that the figure was unconscious. It made no noise as it struck the ground between the fire that had newly blazed up and the fire that still smoldered beyond. Water had collected inside the building, and no dust arose from the fall.

A line of water from one of the pumps arched down on the smoldering fire, and a woman's body suddenly floated up before it: such had been the fall. The body was quite horizontal as it passed through the air. Shimamura started back—not from fear, however. He saw the figure as a phantasm from an unreal world. That stiff figure, flung out into the air, became soft and pliant. With a doll-like passiveness, and the freedom of the lifeless, it seemed to hold both life and death in abeyance. If Shimamura felt even a flicker of uneasiness, it was lest the head drop, or a knee or a hip bend to disturb that perfectly horizontal line. Something of the sort must surely happen; but the body was still horizontal when it struck the ground.

Komako screamed and brought her hands to her eyes. Shimamura gazed at the still form.

When did he realize that it was Yoko? The gasp from the crowd and Komako's scream seemed to come at the same instant; and that instant too there was a suggestion of a spasm in the calf of Yoko's leg, stretched out on the ground.

The scream stabbed him through. At the spasm in Yoko's leg, a chill passed down his spine to his very feet. His heart was pounding in an indefinable anguish.

Yoko's leg moved very slightly, hardly enough to catch the eye.

Even before the spasm passed, Shimamura was looking at the face and the kimono, an arrow figure against a red ground. Yoko had fallen face up. The skirt of her kimono was pulled just over one knee. There was but that slight movement in her leg after she struck the earth. She lay unconscious. For some reason Shimamura did not see death in the still form. He felt rather that Yoko had undergone some shift, some metamorphosis.

Two or three beams from the collapsing balcony were burning over her head. The beautiful eyes that so pierced their object were closed. Her jaw was thrust slightly out, and her throat was arched. The fire flickered over the white face.

Shimamura felt a rising in his chest again as the memory came to him of the night he had been on his way to visit Komako, and he had seen that mountain light shine in Yoko's face. The years and months with Komako seemed to be lighted up in that instant; and there, he knew, was the anguish.

Komako put her hands to her eyes and screamed, and even as the crowd held its breath in that first gasp she broke away from Shimamura and ran toward the fire.

The long geisha's skirts trailing behind her, she staggered through the pools of water and the charred bits of wood that lay scattered over the ground. She turned and struggled back with Yoko at her breast. Her face was strained and desperate, and beneath it Yoko's face hung vacantly, as at the moment of the soul's flight. Komako struggled forward as if she bore her sacrifice, or her punishment.

The crowd found its various voices again. It surged forward to envelop the two.

"Keep back. Keep back, please." He heard Komako's cry. "This girl is insane. She's insane."

He tried to move toward that half-mad voice, but he was pushed aside by the men who had come up to take Yoko from her. As he caught his footing, his head fell back, and the Milky Way flowed down inside him with a roar.

Other Great Names in the Tᴜᴛᴛʟᴇ Cʟᴀssɪᴄs Series

KOBO ABE

The Woman in the Dunes ISBN: 4-8053-0207-0

First published in 1962, this avant-garde work is esteemed as one of the finest Japanese novels of the postwar period, and it was the first of Abe's novels to be translated into English. Niki Jumpei, an amateur entomologist on a weekend trip from the city, comes upon a bizarre village among towering dunes where the residents are living deep within pits. Drawn to assist a widow, he is entrapped and must shovel along with her against the ever-encroaching dunes that threaten to bury the community. While Niki attempts to escape his prison of sand, his relationship with the woman evolves and he comes to accept a whole new identity . . . With striking similarities to the work of Franz Kafka, *The Woman in the Dunes* entices with its unusual plot, its vivid detail, and its existential examination of the human condition.

Secret Rendezvous ISBN: 4-8053-0472-3

In this surrealistic detective story, a man awakens one morning with the groggy recollection that an ambulance had taken his wife from their home in the middle of the night. In his laborious quest to locate her at the hospital, his senses are assaulted by the depraved environment he enters, a labyrinth filled with odd and insane sights, sounds and people.

YUSUNARI KAWABATA

Thousand Cranes ISBN: 4-8053-0667-X

This melancholy tale uses Japan's classical tea ceremony as a backdrop for the relationships between the young man Kikuji and two of his late father's mistresses. Whereas the bitter and domineering Chikako has become as coarse and meddlesome as Kikuji's late father, the beguiling and charming Mrs Ota remains as young and as alluring as ever. Further complicating these relationships is Mrs Ota's 20-year-old daughter, Fumiko. Kikuji retraces his father's fickle footsteps as he tries to escape the domineering Chikako while harboring a guilty passion for Mrs Ota, and Fumiko's efforts to intervene ultimately lead to the novel's stunning climax. Kawabata deftly employs the symbolism of the Japanese tea ceremony as well as the minimalist style of *sumi-e*, *haiku*, and Noh theater in this exploration of sex, love, guilt, and raw revenge.

YUKIO MISHIMA

After the Banquet   ISBN: 4-8053-0628-9

Kazu is a successful, independent woman determined never to fall in love again—that is, until a former government cabinet minister walks into her life. Attracted despite herself by Noguchi's aristocratic background and intellectualism, she marries him—even as the wide social and moral gulf between them signals catastrophe. In her own selfish attempt to resurrect Noguchi's political career, Kazu secretly funds his idealistic campaign, but Noguchi finds out and is morally offended. Now Kazu has to decide: should she comply with her husband's strict code of conduct, or return to the independent life she'd once cherished? The climax of this tale reveals Mishima's full range of power as a master storyteller and novelist.

Forbidden Colors   ISBN: 4-8053-0630-0

Widely regarded as Mishima's finest work, *Forbidden Colors* explores the issue of sexual hedonism in postwar Japan. An aging, embittered novelist employs the beautiful and young Yuichi Minami to avenge himself on the women who have betrayed him. As his mentor forces him into a loveless marriage and a string of meaningless love affairs, Yuichi looks for physical and emotional solace in Japan's vast gay underworld. As he works his way through the gay world's secret spaces, Yuichi meets with blackmailers, pimps and male prostitutes, soon finds himself as vulnerable and defenseless as the women he preyed on.

SOSEKI NATSUME

And Then   ISBN: 0-8048-1537-2

One of Natsume Soseki's most admired works, *And Then* is a novel of love and disillusionment that tells the story of a young man for whom idleness has become an expression of rebellion. Having become thoroughly alienated by the cultural upheaval in Japan, Daisuke has lost the values to guide his life. Yet his refined indifference to everything is completely disrupted when he falls in love with his best friend's wife. Now for the first time, Daisuke must choose his own fate.

Kokoro   ISBN: 4-8053-0161-9

Set in the turbulent Meiji era, a chance encounter on a Kamakura beach irrevocably links a young student to a man he simply calls "Sensei." Intrigued by Sensei's aloofness and wanting to know more about him, the student calls upon Sensei with increasing frequency. Eventually, Sensei and his beautiful wife open up their home and their lives to him. The young man graduates from university and is called home to his dying father, but the Sensei draws him back to Tokyo with a letter of heartfelt confession . . . Written in 1914, *Kokoro* provides a timeless psychological analysis of one man's alienation from society, and starkly but gently shows the depth of both friendship and love.

JUNICHIRO TANIZAKI

Some Prefer Nettles   ISBN: 4-8053-0633-5

The conflict between traditional and modern Japanese culture is at the heart of this novel. Kaname is a smug, modern man living in a modern marriage. He gamely allows his wife to become the lover of another man, an act that does not cure the profound sadness at the heart of their relationship. So Kaname gradually retreats into the protection of traditional rituals, attitudes and tastes, eventually making love to O-Hisa, his father-in-law's old-fashioned mistress, as he abandons the modern world entirely. The novel's other characters, including Kaname's wife, his lover, his father-in-law, and even the cities in which they live, all symbolize the modern and ancient ways of life in Japan. Tanizaki's characteristic irony, eroticism, and psychological undertones make *Some Prefer Nettles* an exceptional and compelling read.

The Key   ISBN: 4-8053-0632-7

In *The Key*, a middle-aged husband and his wife both seek passion outside of their loveless marriage, telling their stories in the form of parallel diary entries. The novel carefully explores the theme of sexual desire, and Tanizaki's restrained and delicate prose artfully conveys not only the consequences of the couple's pursuits, but also demonstrates the very best of Japanese literature.

❧❧❧ TUTTLE CLASSICS ❧❧❧

LITERATURE

ABE, Kobo　安部公房
The Box Man　箱男　4-8053-0395-6
The Face of Another　他人の顔　4-8053-0120-1
Inter Ice Age 4　第四間氷期　4-8053-0268-2
Secret Rendezvous　密会　4-8053-0472-3
The Woman in the Dunes　砂の女　4-8053-0207-0

AKUTAGAWA, Ryunosuke　芥川龍之介
Japanese Short Stories　芥川龍之介短編集　4-8053-0464-2
Kappa　河童　0-8048-3251-X
Rashomon and Other Stories　羅生門　0-8048-1457-0

ATODA, Takashi　阿刀田高
The Square Persimmon and Other Stories　四角い柿　0-8048-1644-1

DAZAI, Osamu　太宰治
Crackling Mountain and Other Stories　太宰治短編集　0-8048-3342-7
No Longer Human　人間失格　4-8053-0756-0
The Setting Sun　斜陽　4-8053-0672-6

EDOGAWA, Rampo　江戸川乱歩
Japanese Tales of Mystery & Imagination　乱歩短編集　0-8048-0319-6

ENDO, Shusaku　遠藤周作
Deep River　深い河　0-8048-2013-9
The Final Martyrs　最後の殉教者　4-8053-0625-4
Foreign Studies　留学　0-8048-1626-3
The Golden Country　黄金の国　0-8048-3337-0
A Life of Jesus　イエスの生涯　4-8053-0668-8
Scandal　スキャンダル　0-8048-1558-5
Stained Glass Elegies　短編集　4-8053-0624-6
The Sea and Poison　海と毒薬　4-8053-0330-1
Volcano　火山　4-8053-0664-5
When I Whistle　口笛を吹くとき　4-8053-0627-0
Wonderful Fool　おバカさん　4-8053-0376-X

TUTTLE CLASSICS

HEARN, Lafcadio　ラフカディオ・ハーン

In Ghostly Japan　霊の日本　0-8048-3361-2 (4-8053-0749-8 for sale
  in Japan only)

Kokoro　心　0-8048-3660-4 (4-8053-0748-X for sale in Japan only)

Kwaidan　怪談　0-8048-3662-0 (4-8053-0750-1 for sale in Japan only)

INOUE, Yasushi　井上靖

The Counterfeiter and Other Stories　ある偽作家の生涯、他
  0-8048-3252-8

The Hunting Gun　猟銃　0-8048-0257-2

ISHIKAWA, Takuboku　石川啄木

Romaji Diary and Sad Toys　ローマ字日記、悲しき玩具
  0-8048-3253-6

KAIKO, Takeshi　開高健

Darkness in Summer　夏の闇　0-8048-3325-7 (4-8053-0644-0
  for sale in Japan only)

KAWABATA, Yasunari　川端康成

Beauty and Sadness　美しさと哀しみと　4-8053-0394-8

The Izu Dancer and Other Stories　伊豆の踊り子　0-8048-1141-5
  (4-8053-0744-7 for sale in Japan only)

The Master of Go　名人　4-8053-0673-4

The Old Capital　古都　4-8053-0610-6

Snow Country　雪国　4-8053-0635-1

The Sound of the Mountain　山の音　4-8053-0663-7

Thousand Cranes　千羽鶴　4-8053-0667-X

MISHIMA, Yukio　三島由紀夫

After the Banquet　宴のあと　4-8053-0628-9

Confessions of a Mask　仮面の告白　4-8053-0232-1

Death in Midsummer and Other Stories　真夏の死　4-8053-0617-3

The Decay of the Angel　天人五衰　4-8053-0385-9

Forbidden Colors　禁色　4-8053-0630-0

Runaway Horses　奔馬　4-8053-0354-9

The Sailor Who Fell from Grace with the Sea　午後の曳航
  4-8053-0629-7

The Samurai Ethics and Modern Japan　葉隠入門　4-8053-0645-9

The Sound of Waves　潮騒　4-8053-0636-X

TUTTLE CLASSICS

Spring Snow　春の雪　4-8053-0327-1

The Temple of Dawn　暁の寺　4-8053-0373-5

The Temple of the Golden Pavilion　金閣寺　4-8053-0637-8

Thirst for Love　愛の渇き　4-8053-0634-3

MIURA, Ayako　三浦綾子

Shiokari Pass　塩狩峠　0-8048-1529-1

MORI, Ogai　森鴎外

Vita Sexualis　ヰタ・セクスアリス　0-8048-1048-6

Wild Geese　雁　0-8048-1070-2

NAGAI, Kafu　永井荷風

A Strange Tale from East of the River and Other Stories　墨東綺譚
4-8053-0266-6

NATSUME, Soseki　夏目漱石

And Then　それから　0-8048-1537-2

Botchan　坊ちゃん　0-8048-3703-1 (4-8053-0802-8 for sale in
Japan only)

Grass on the Wayside　道草　4-8053-0258-5

The Heredity of Taste　趣味の遺伝　0-8048-3602-7 (4-8053-0766-8
for sale in Japan only)

Kokoro　こころ　4-8053-0746-3

I am a Cat　吾輩は猫である　0-8048-3265-X

Inside My Grass Doors　硝子戸の中　0-8048-3312-5

The Miner　坑夫　0-8048-1577-1

Mon　門　4-8053-0291-7

My Individualism and The Philosophical Foundations of Literature
私の個人主義、文芸の哲学的基礎　0-8048-3603-5 (4-8053-0767-6
for sale in Japan only)

Spring Miscellany　永日小品　0-8048-3326-5

Ten Nights of Dream, Hearing Things, The Heredity of Taste
夢十夜、他　0-8048-3329-X (4-8053-0658-0 for sales Japan only)

The Three-Cornered World　草枕　4-8053-0201-1

To The Spring Equinox and Beyond　彼岸過迄　0-8048-3328-1
(4-8053-0741-2 for sales Japan only)

The 210th Day　二百十日　0-8048-3320-6

The Wayfarer　行人　4-8053-0204-6

TUTTLE CLASSICS

NIWA, Fumio　丹羽文雄
The Buddha Tree　菩提樹　0-8048-3254-4

OE, Kenzaburo　大江健三郎
A Personal Matter　個人的な体験　4-8053-0641-6

OOKA, Shohei　大岡昇平
Fires on the Plain　野火　0-8048-1379-5

OSARAGI, Jiro　大佛次郎
The Journey　旅路　0-8048-3255-2

SAWAMURA, Sadako　沢村貞子
My Asakusa　私の浅草　0-8048-2135-6

SETOUCHI, Harumi　瀬戸内晴美
Beauty in Disarray　美は乱調にあり 0-8048-3322-2 (4-8053-0747-1
　for sale in Japan only)

SHIGA, Naoya　志賀直哉
The Paper Door and Other Stories 襖、他　0-8048-1893-2

SUMII, Sue　住井すゑ
The River With No Bridge　橋のない川　0-8048-3327-3

TAKEYAMA, Michio　竹山道雄
Harp of Burma　ビルマの竪琴　0-8048-0232-7

TANIZAKI, Junichiro　谷崎潤一郎
Diary of a Mad Old Man　瘋癲老人日記　4-8053-0675-0
The Key　鍵　4-8053-0632-7
The Makioka Sisters　細雪　4-8053-0670-X
Naomi　痴人の愛　0-8048-1520-8
The Secret History of the Lord of Musashi and Arrowroot
　武州公秘話、吉野葛　4-8053-0657-2
Seven Japanese Tales　谷崎潤一郎短編集　4-8053-0640-8
Some Prefer Nettles　蓼喰う虫　4-8053-0633-5

TATEMATSU, Wahei　立松和平
Distant Thunder　遠雷　0-8048-2120-8

UCHIDA, Yasuo　内田康夫
The Togakushi Legend Murders　戸隠伝説殺人事件　0-8048-3554-3

UNO, Chiyo　宇野千代
Confessions of Love　色ざんげ　4-8053-0613-0